THE DOOR

Y I Lee

This is a work of fiction. Any resemblance to actual
people or places is coincidental.

Cover image from an original painting by Y I Lee
Cover design by Rebecca Fyfe

Chapter 1

Standing in the kitchen doorway, Renee frowned as she discreetly watched her sister. Slumped in her chair by the fire, Cadi's blond hair, emphasised her pale complexion, she looked frail and vulnerable. The ache in Renee's chest deepened. *How could someone, once so full of life, suddenly become sick and in need of constant care.*

The sound of the kettle switching off distracted Renee. Sighing softly, she poured boiling water into a coffee pot, and put it on the tray with the mugs. Her lips softened in a smile as the delicious aroma of fresh coffee permeated the kitchen. Carrying the tray into the lounge, she glanced through the glass doors into the studio. Bathed in the soft glow of a setting sun, the studio looked strangely ethereal.

"I can't believe how quickly this afternoon has gone," she said, placing the tray on the small side table. "It's a shame we couldn't spend the whole day together."

Cadi glanced up, her blue eyes crinkled in a smile. "I know, but I'm grateful nurse Emery was happy to bring me here; even if only for a few hours while she visits her mother."

"Does she have any other family?" Renee asked.

"Not as far as I know. She's only ever mentioned her elderly mother."

Taking her mug, she slowly sipped the hot brew.

Renee watched her, noticing the slight tremble in her hand as she held the mug to her lips. "It shouldn't be too hot, but be careful," she warned. Renee discreetly looked away. Chewing her lip, she quenched the tears pricking the back of her eyes. The word she'd grown to loath rolled around in her head...why? Aware of the pain in her jaw, she unclenched her teeth, and took an inaudible breath. Sitting back in her chair she watched the flickering fire light reflect on her sister's pale, almost translucent skin. "So, how are you?" she asked softly. "It seems ages since we last saw each other." Anxious, and not sure what to do with her hands, Renee gripped her mug. The heat helped her focus.

"Oh, you know me; I take the good with the bad. The medication nurse Emery gives me isn't doing much to help. But on the whole, I'm not too bad. I even managed to do a little gardening the other day."

Her sister's positivity brought a fleeting smile to Renee's face. "I wish we could spend more time together."

"Me too, I do miss you."

Latching onto Cadi's words, Renee jumped in with both feet. "So why do you have to stay in that huge house miles from anywhere? You could live here with me." Seeing her sister draw back and shake her head, Renee glanced away and tried to swallow the ache in her throat. *How many times have we had this conversation?*

"You know why, Renee." Cadi's voice trembled with emotion. "I love that house. It's full of memories…happy memories of my life with Ted, short though it was." Pausing, she stared into the fire. In a voice hardly audible, she said. "I feel Ted's presence there, so strongly. I have to stay. I need to be near him. I can't leave." Fixing Renee with her large blue eyes, she said softly. "Please, Renee, try to understand. I will never leave Five Acres. Having nurse Emery with me has made it possible for me to stay in the home I love. I need her and she is good to me."

Kneeling beside her, Renee took her sisters hand…flinching at the coldness of her skin. She gave it a reassuring squeeze. "Believe me Cadi I'm glad you have her. I know she was there for you when Ted died." Pausing, she pursed her lips. "I wish I could have come to his funeral and stayed with you for a while, but it all happened so quickly and with the exhibition in New York, I just couldn't get back in time, I'm so—"

"Stop fretting, it's okay I understand. Your art is your life and your work. The last thing I want is to drag you away. I am well looked after with Emery and Stella, so please stop worrying."

Her warm smile reassured Renee. "I know, but it's a shame it all happened while I was abroad. But it's not only my work. When mother passed away and left me this house, I felt I should stay. Actually, I wanted to stay, this was our home." *If you had not married we would be here together.* As the thought entered her head she grimaced and chewed her lip.

Seeing a tear trickle down Cadi's face, Renee gently wiped it away, and embraced her. Her body felt so frail. "Please don't upset yourself. You're all I have now." Pulling away, Renee gazed at her. "You live so far away, and I worry about you. Is that so wrong of me?"

"Of course not," Cadi said. Taking the proffered tissue, she blew her nose. "You're all I have too."

Encouraged by her words, Renee quickly said, "If you stayed here with me, nurse Emery could still look after you. There's plenty of room," she said, using her arm to emphasise the point.

Seeing the dark flush on Cadi's cheeks, she moved away and sat in the chair opposite. "I'm doing it again, aren't I? Sorry."

Glancing at her, Cadi said firmly, "Let's not discuss it further."

Hearing the tension in her voice, Renee nodded.

"Ted is with me in that house. His presence keeps me going. The only way I will leave is in a coffin."

The fleeting darkness in her blue eyes, made the hair lift on the back of Renee's neck. "Okay," she said raising her hands. "I won't mention it again."

"Good," Cadi said. "Now show me the painting. I can't wait to see it."

Her sister's sudden change of attitude was a relief; nevertheless it threw Renee for a moment. Without a word, she helped Cadi out of her chair, and led her into the studio. "Wait there a moment, and I'll fetch it."

Resting the painting on the easel, Renee turned to Cadi. It was hard to gauge her sister's expression, but from the sparkle in her eyes, Renee guessed she liked it. "What do think?"

Moving closer, Cadi studied the painting. "It's brilliant, I love the door, it's so gothic. You know me; I've always loved anything gothicy."

Renee couldn't help a chuckle. "Gothicy! Where do you find these strange words?"

"It not a strange word," Cadi insisted. "It expresses the door perfectly."

Staring at the painting, Renee could see what she meant. In the subdued light, and with the vague impression of a figure in the window, it did look a little spooky. The setting sun bathed the studio in a strange glow, somehow intensifying the gothic feel of the painting. With this particular work, Renee had allowed herself the luxury of darker expression. She was known for atmospheric artwork, but this was different, with this work, somehow she'd plumbed a deeper depth. Sorrow over her sister's sudden illness had driven…inspired her. The outcome, she found strangely perplexing. Why did the door seem familiar?

Renee allowed her eyes to rove over the painting. The small leaded window echoed the shape of the old ivy covered door. She had no idea why, but old doors fascinated her…drew her. She loved rusting hinges and heavy ornate bolts. It had taken her months to complete the painting; most of that time spent reproducing a door as old and battered as one might find in an ancient deserted castle.

Even as she painted it, in the back of her mind she'd thought of her sister. Like Renee, Cadi loved old doors and ancient buildings. Before Cadi's marriage to Ted, they'd spent many happy days wandering around National Trust properties, the older the better.

Cadi's long sigh broke her reverie. Taking her sister's arm, Renee guided her to the small wicker chair. "Here sit down, are you alright?" Cadi's pale skin and the dark shadows under her eyes worried Renee.

"I'm fine, stop fussing." Raising a shaky hand she touched Renee's arm. "Are you sure you want me to have the painting? It would be an awesome addition to your next exhibition."

"I'm quite sure. I painted it for you." Gently, she squeezed her hand. "It will remind you of all the wonderful old doors we've seen on our travels." Seeing the sparkle in her sister's eyes was all the thanks she needed. "That's settled then," she said, getting to her feet. "You can take it with you and get nurse Emery to hang it. What room will you put—?"

"It's going in the library," Cadi said, before Renee could finish the question.

Smiling, Renee glanced at the painting. "I'm sure it will look wonderful in there."

Cadi nodded. "I'm going to hang it over the fireplace. The light there is perfect." She paused, and lowered her head, the knuckles of her hands whitened as she gripped the sides of her chair.

"What is it?" Renee asked. "Are you in pain?"

Shaking her head, Cadi said in a voice choked with emotion. "No, it's just that whenever I go into the library, it's as if Ted is there waiting for me. The feeling gets stronger each time I go in the room."

Renee's stomach churned, taking her sister's outstretched hand it was hard to know what to say, Cadi was fragile, vulnerable.

Ted had been unwell for some time. He was a good few years older than Cadi, but his sudden heart attack eight months ago had shaken them all. Cadi had adored him. They were as close as any couple could be. Renee often wondered if the shock of losing Ted had brought on her illness. His sudden passing had left her bereft in so many ways. "He's not really there, Cadi," Renee said gently. "He's gone."

"So why do I feel his presence so strongly. Sometimes, I can even smell his aftershave." Her expression darkened as she stared at her sister. "You're a Christian, you believe in the afterlife, so help me to understand."

"I'm sorry, Cadi. Just because I'm a believer, doesn't mean I have all the answers. There are many things I don't understand, and this is one of them. I wish I could help you. I wish I understood myself."

Watching Cadi slump in her chair, Renee blinked away tears. Kneeling beside the chair, she gently rubbed her sister's arm. "Ted was a believer. Did he ever speak to you about these things?"

Raising her head, Cadi stared at Renee. "Yes, he did, constantly. He tried so hard to make me understand."

Maybe, he tried too hard. Renee dismissed the thought.

"Every day he would say, God loves you, Cadi." Her face creased in a dark frown, tears streamed down her cheeks. With a trembling hand she wiped them away. "If He loves me why did He take Ted, and why am I sick?"

Renee wrapped her arms around her sister and held her close. She had no words. There was nothing she could say.

Pulling away, Cadi stared into her face. "Ted said if I believed, we would be together for ever. Is that true, Renee?"

Hearing the pain in her sister's voice, and held in her questioning gaze, Renee cringed. Nodding, she said softly, "Yes it is."

Looking at the painting on the easel, Cadi said softly…so softly, Renee could hardly hear her. "There's an old door in the corner of our library? The house has a few original doors, but Ted knew the one in the library was my favourite." She paused.

Seeing the sad, thoughtful expression on her face, Renee waited.

Cadi returned her sister's gaze. "I could never understand why it was always locked. Why do you think that was?" She didn't wait for a response. "Actually, the door in your painting is not dissimilar to the one in the library."

Renee smiled at her. "I'm glad."

Cadi took her hand. "Ted used to say, that if he died before me. I was to imagine he'd simply gone through that door and was on the other side waiting for me." Lowering her head, she chewed on her lip. "How can I go to him if the door is always locked? I wish I could open it and go through, but I can't find the key. I've looked everywhere, but it's useless, and now I'm unwell I just don't have the strength to continue the search. It's in the library somewhere, I know it is." Wiping a tear from her cheek, she gazed at the painting.

Renee wanted to question her...make helpful suggestions, but seeing her sister's emotional state, decided against it.

Cadi wrapped her arms around Renee's neck. "Thank you for letting me have the painting."

"I'll wrap it for you," Renee said, slowly easing out of Cadi's embrace. "You can take it with you when you leave." Cadi's teary smile touched Renee's heart. Holding her emotions in check, she asked. "When will nurse Emery be here?"

Cadi glanced at her watch. "Soon, so I guess I'd better get ready, I don't want to hold her up."

"No, it was good of her to bring you here. So we'd best not keep her waiting, you have a long journey home."

৩৩৩

Supporting Cadi by the arm, Renee guided her towards the car. Gravel crunched under their feet, intruding on the silence between them.

"I wish you didn't have to go," Renee whispered.

"I know, but I must."

Nurse Emery stood by the car, her arm resting on the open door, her fingers tapping impatiently on the door frame, but as she watched them approach her face softened in a smile. Stepping forward, she took Cadi by the arm, and settled her in the passenger seat. Leaving her to fix the seat belt she hurried to the rear of the car and put the painting in the boot.

Renee followed her. "Thank you for bringing my sister to see me, and for taking care of her."

The nurse's quick smile, made her grey eyes twinkle. "You're welcome," she said.

Knowing Cadi couldn't hear, Renee asked, "Do you enjoy working for my sister? I only ask, as it must be lonely for you living miles away from anywhere."

"I'm perfectly happy, thank you," the nurse said. "Your sister and I get on extremely well." Sliding into the driver's seat, she closed the car door and wound the window down. "We need to go Renee, it's a long way home, but I hope we see you again soon." With that, she started the car and gunned the engine. Gravel sprayed as the car roared down the long gravel drive.

Shaking her head, Renee couldn't help thinking. *I hope she doesn't drive like that all the way home.* Her stomach rolled uncomfortably as she watched the vehicle disappear.

Walking into the house, she cringed at the silence. *Go on, admit it, you're lonely.* Those silent words made her think, brought her up short. Slumping in a chair she rested her chin in her hands, consoling herself with the thought, that loneliness wasn't her only motive.

Renee loved her baby sister, she always had. The wide gap in their ages had never really mattered. They both had so much in common. Deep down Renee knew, Cadi would be better off living with her. After all Swindon was where they were brought up. As kids they had loved to roam the Wiltshire countryside on their bikes, enjoying the long hot summer days.

Frowning, she massaged her aching temples. *Why did Ted have to take her all the way to Northumberland? Right to the border of Scotland, no less!* Inwardly, she groaned. *All the facilities she needs are here in Swindon. I'm sure the hospital would find out what's wrong with her.*

Pinching her lips together she tried to keep resentment for Ted at bay, reminding herself he was a good man, who had cared deeply for her sister. Nevertheless, the large age gap between them, and Ted's health issues had always concerned Renee, and even more so their mother.

Thinking of her mother brought hot tears to her eyes. In many ways Renee was glad she had passed away, unaware her youngest daughter was sick. Renee knew she would never have coped.

Weary with emotion, she rose from her chair and put the coffee pot and mugs on the tray. Carrying it into the kitchen, she placed it on the table and went to the sink. Staring into the darkness, she embraced the silence. Glancing at the clock on the wall, Renee was surprised to see it was already seven thirty. *Too early to go to bed*, she thought. Stifling a yawn she wandered into the studio, hoping if she worked on her latest painting, it would tire her enough to sleep. Switching on the light, she placed the canvas on the easel. In an instant, she thought of the door painting…thought of her sister's long journey home.

I wonder where they are. A long way from home yet, I guess. Sighing, she squeezed some acrylic paint onto her pallet. "I hope Cadi keeps her promise and rings me when they arrive." Her voice, though quiet, echoed in the sparsely furnished studio. Even though she lived alone, Renee was not one for talking to herself. *It's when you start answering back there's a problem,* she thought. Her lips flickered in a smile.

Rotating her neck, she tried to ease the tension in her shoulders. The silence unnerved her, so she switched on the radio. It was set to classic FM. Instantly she relaxed, as the wonderful strains of a piano concerto filled the room. Taking a brush loaded with paint she soon lost herself in her artwork and the inspiring music.

Losing track of time, the strident sound of the phone startled her. Glancing at the clock she saw it was ten thirty. Grabbing the phone she pressed it to her ear. It was late, but she prayed it was her sister's promised call, "Cadi?"

"No, sorry this is nurse Emery. Cadi has retired for the night. She found the long journey taxing."

Trying to hide the anxious tremble in her voice, Renee asked. "Is she alright?"

"Yes she's fine, but as I say she found the journey taxing. I'm sure she will be in touch when she is rested."

"Please, get her to ring me tomorrow, and give her my love."

"I will don't worry."

The nurse's voice sounded distant, as though she were already putting the phone down. Sure enough Renee heard a click and loud buzzing in her ear. Sighing, she dropped her brushes into a jar of water, and decided to go to bed. *At least I can relax now. Cadi is safely home.* Switching off the lights she made her way upstairs. Standing at the bedroom window, she paused before closing the drapes. At the bottom of the large garden, the moon hung like a huge silver disk. Its soft light illuminated the room, so much so, Renee decided to leave the drapes open and got ready for bed.

Snuggled under the cosy duvet, she stared round the room. Apart from a few shadows, it was almost as bright as day. *A bombers moon*, she thought. Punching her feather pillow, she buried her head in its softness and closed her eyes. Downstairs, her mother's old grandfather clock chimed eleven before settling into its loud rhythmic tick. The familiar sound reverberated through the house, lulling Renee into a restless sleep. Her dreams filled with visions of her sister, and a rustic old door.

Chapter 2

The insistent ringing of the phone roused Renee, bleary eyed she glanced at the clock, it was eight thirty. Still half asleep, she groped around the bedside cabinet until her fingers found the noisy instrument. In a voice thick from sleep she murmured, "Hello." Hearing her sister's voice nudged her sleepy brain into gear. Leaning against the headboard, she smiled and said. "You sound perky this morning. Have you recovered from the journey?"

"Yes, sorry about last night, by the time we got home, I was simply pooped and had to go straight to bed. Sorry to ring you at this hour, I know you're not an early riser."

Renee smiled, Cadi knew her well! Even as a child, Renee loved her bed. "Don't worry it's not that early. I'm pleased to hear from you."

"Well I promised I'd ring. Thanks for yesterday. I enjoyed spending time with you."

It was on the tip of Renee's tongue to say, *if you lived closer we could do it more often*, but she curbed it, not wishing to upset her sister. Changing the subject, she asked. "When will you hang the painting?"

She could hear the excitement in Cadi's voice as she said. "Nurse Emery is doing it now. Can you hear the banging?"

"No, but I'm sure she'll do a good job."

"Indeed she will. She's as good as your average handy man."

Renee laughed, "I'm sure she is. I can't wait to see how the painting looks on your wall."

"Nor can I. Emery is going to help me downstairs in a minute. I'm dying to see it." After a momentary silence, there was a smile in her voice, as she said. "She's here, so I'll ring you this evening and tell you how it looks."

"Okay, speak to you later." The hollow sound as the phone went dead left Renee with an unpleasant gutted feeling…a feeling she couldn't explain. "I need coffee," she muttered as she scrambled out of bed and grabbed her dressing gown.

Renee plodded downstairs into the kitchen. Late summer sunshine streamed through the small window above the sink. She stood there for a moment enjoying the warmth while waiting for the kettle to boil. Staring out of the window, her brown eyes creased in a smile as she gazed at her expansive garden. It looked beautiful, a tranquil forest of emerald. As an artist, she never ceased to be amazed at the numerous shades of green, each shade blending and complimenting the other. In contrast, a beautiful array of wild flowers swayed in the morning breeze.

Sniffing, Renee brushed away a tear. "What's the matter with me?" Her voice seemed to echo in the quiet of the house. Her hand shook slightly as she put ground coffee in the carafe. She knew the answer to the question. *My sister should be here with me…safe. She would love it, I know she would, but how do I convince her?* Slumped at the kitchen table, Renee sipped her coffee, hoping the strong sweet brew would rouse her fuzzy mind, it did, but she still had no clear answer. How could she convince Cadi to come and join her?

Leaving her mug in the sink, she went upstairs for a shower. Sighing with pleasure, she stood under the hot water letting it run through her long auburn hair and cascade over her shoulders, enjoying the sensation as it pummelled the tension out of her muscles. Standing there with her eyes closed, an idea popped into her head. Switching the shower off, she grabbed a large towel and hurried into the bedroom, smiling at the trail of wet footprints. *Stupid woman, you should have dried your feet.* She didn't care, her head buzzed with an idea and she wanted to get things moving as soon as possible.

Swathed in the bath towel she curled up on the bed and made a phone call. After a few moments, she put the phone down, and relaxed on her pillows. Her body tingled with excitement. *Don't you just love it when a plan comes together!*

Her one woman show in the local gallery was booked for two months ahead, but she desperately needed to bring it forward. Much to her surprise, an artist had cancelled and the gallery were able to offer her their slot. To say she was delighted was an understatement. Her nearest neighbour, who lived two miles away, could have heard her gleeful whoops.

So now, instead of two months, Renee had three weeks in which to get her work ready, plus finish the painting she was still working on. Scrambling into her working clothes, she decided to have a quick breakfast and get cracking. "Thank goodness I work in Acrylics," she said as she clattered downstairs to the kitchen. Wolfing down a bowl of cereal she hurried into the studio. The incentive to have everything ready on time worked like a spur, urging her on and filling her with inspiration.

The painting on the easel had given her nothing but trouble from the start, but now, all of sudden, it flowed, and in no time it was finished. Resting her hands on her hips, Renee surveyed the finished work. It was good. She'd achieved what she wanted. Smiling, she flopped exhausted into the small wicker chair.

Narrowing her eyes, she studied the painting in the mirror. It was her favourite technique for checking perspective, and it never failed her.

Feeling the stiffness in her neck, she raised her arms and enjoyed a good long stretch. Her contented sigh was eclipsed by the loud rumble from her stomach. "Time for some lunch, I think, or should that be dinner?" Walking into the kitchen Renee proceeded to find something to eat. As she rooted through the fridge, the old grandfather clock chimed. Glancing at her watch, her eyebrows rose in surprise, it was already three o'clock. "Good grief!" She grumbled. "Where does time go?"

She was hungry, but not enough to cook. Anticipating her sister's call, and the exciting news she wanted to share with her, dampened her appetite. Her hands trembled as she prepared a cheese and tomato toasty. Putting the mug of coffee and the plate of food on a tray, she carried it back to the studio. Renee felt a pleasant lightness as she sat in her chair, she loved this room. It was her place of creativity, her place of peace. Smiling, she nibbled the toasty and stared out at the garden.

Having finished her rather late lunch she felt relaxed. Leaning back in the chair, she closed her eyes for a moment. Outside in the garden the birds were singing, a blackbird's song floated on the air. Enjoying the relative silence, she thanked God for His help with the various areas she needed to sort out, especially the gallery. The fact they were able to accommodate her request to change exhibition dates, was a relief.

However, a nervous fluttering in her chest succeeded in stifling her assurance. Groaning with frustration she stood to her feet and paced the floor.

Renee tried to ignore the negative thoughts, but they persisted. *Everything's arranged, but what if Cadi doesn't like my idea. What if …?* The doubts lingered, refusing to go away.

಄ ಄ ಄

Cadi relaxed in the luxurious softness of her husband's office chair. Leaning her head back, she focused on the painting. It filled the space above the fireplace perfectly; in fact its presence dominated the library. With half closed eyes, Cadi studied it. The similarity between the door in the painting and the small door in the corner of the room, took her breath away…made her skin tingle. Illuminated in soft lamp light, the painting held her attention, drew her in. Cadi found it hard to look away. However, a soft tap on the library door broke the spell. Turning her head, Cadi smiled as nurse Emery entered the library.

Emery frowned. "Are you still staring at that painting?"

Cadi nodded. "I love it."

"So it would seem." Tutting, Emery placed a tray on the desk. "If you can tear yourself away, I asked Stella to make you scrambled eggs on toast, I know you like it."

Pulling the tray closer, Cadi lifted the stainless steel warmer off the plate. "Ooh lovely, she's put some cheese in the eggs, thanks Emery."

The nurse smiled. "You're welcome. Eat it before it goes cold. Are you warm enough in here?" Emery asked walking over to the fireplace. Grasping the small ornate shovel she placed fresh coal on the fire, topping it off with a large pine log. "There you are, once that catches it will warm up."

Resting her hand on the mantel shelf she stared round the room. The wood panelled library, with its heavy furniture and row upon row of musty books, was not her favourite room in the house. However, with the drapes pulled, and the fire blazing in the hearth, it looked and felt surprisingly cosy. Walking to the library door, she paused. "Ring for me, when you've finished your supper, and I'll fetch the tray. Oh, and don't forget you have to phone your sister."

"I will," Cadi said through a mouthful of egg. Closing her eyes she relished the cheesy taste. Finishing her eggs, she pushed the tray aside and grabbed the phone.

Hearing Renee's news, the contagious excitement in her voice, Cadi couldn't help chuckling as she replaced the receiver. She was still smiling when she rang the bell for Emery. "My sister is coming to stay," she exclaimed as Emery entered the library. "Can you ask Stella to sort out a guest room for me?" Tilting her head, Cadi stared at the nurse, the woman's lack of response, puzzled her. "Did you hear—?"

"Sorry, yes I heard you. Which room will she be staying in?"

Cadi rose to her feet, a thoughtful frown creasing her brow. "We'll put her in the rose room, the one next to mine. She'll love it and the view is gorgeous."

"When is she coming?" Emery asked.

"In about four weeks, I believe." Grinning and rubbing her hands together, Cadi flopped in the comfy armchair by the fire.

Emery put Cadi's empty plate on the tray and walked to the door. Pausing she turned, "Will you be retiring soon? I only ask as you need to take your medication before you go to sleep."

Pursing her lips, Cadi muttered. "I wish I didn't have to take that wretched stuff."

"I'm afraid you must, doctors' orders. We must keep your condition under control."

"Exactly what is my condition? I wish I knew what was wrong with me."

"Don't worry, the doctors will find out soon. You look tired. I suggest you go to bed. I'll bring the medication up shortly."

With a weary sigh, Cadi rose to her feet and followed Emery into the expansive hallway. Sitting on the stair lift, she pressed the button and sat back. She would never have believed at her young age, she would be unable to climb a flight of stairs.

The stair lift had been put in for Ted, when his heart condition was first diagnosed. Cadi hated it. At the time she felt it ruined the elegant flow of the Georgian staircase. But since being ill herself, she'd come to realise what a benefit it had been to her husband, and now to herself. When at first she was forced to use it, she complained hotly. "It's so slow. I could walk up faster!"

"But that's the point, you can't," nurse Emery had said.

Noting nurse Emery's raised brows, and the amused twinkle in her eyes, Cadi had laughed. Relaxing on the slow moving chair, she let her eyes rove over the numerous paintings adorning the walls. They were mostly of family members, with an occasional landscape hanging among them.

Reaching the landing, the chair stopped. For a moment Cadi stayed where she was, her eyes fixed on a large oil painting hanging on the opposite wall. Her husband's warm dark eyes stared down at her. He was a younger man, vigorous, and in his prime. Staring at his handsome chiselled face, Cadi couldn't halt her tears. *I wish I'd known him then.*

Nurse Emery's heavy footfall on the stairs broke the moment. Struggling out of the chair, Cadi wiped away her tears, and slowly made her way down the long hallway to her room. Glancing back, she smiled at Emery following close behind, her footsteps muffled by the thick pile of the pale cream carpet.

Striding past her, Emery reached Cadi's door, opened it and stood aside. "There we are. Get yourself to bed, you look tired. Will you need any help?"

Cadi shook her head, "No, I can manage thank you."

"Very well, here's your medication, I'll put it by your bed. Don't forget to take it."

Kicking off her shoes, Cadi watched the nurse stride from the room. Sitting on the side of the bed, her breathing accelerated. The glass, half full of cloudy water filled her vision, she gave an involuntary shudder. Picking it up, she studied it. "I don't know what good this is. I certainly don't feel any better in fact sometimes I feel worse." Her hand shook as she swallowed it.

Emery had already turned down the bed and closed the drapes. With a weary sigh, Cadi perched on the side of the bed and stared round the room. She loved it. Soft lamp light accentuated the pale blue walls. Cream drapes embellished with tiny bluebells, concealed her favourite feature in the whole room, a deep window seat. She loved to curl among the cushions and read, or gaze out of the window.

The large Georgian house sat in acres of wild Northumberland countryside. Their only neighbour for miles around...cattle and sheep, and an occasional deer.

Sitting on the bed Cadi listened to the silence. She knew if it weren't for Emery and Stella Jones, the housekeeper, she would die of loneliness.

Cadi loved Stella. From the first day Ted introduced them, the two women gelled. Stella had been with Ted a number of years, long before he married Cadi. Ted's illness and sudden death affected Stella greatly. In their shared grief the two women clung to each other.

"Please don't leave me," Cadi had begged her. She was terrified Stella would walk out, especially since the house keeper disliked nurse Emery.

Stella had bemoaned the nurse's presence from the first day she crossed the threshold. "We don't need her," she said to Cadi on numerous occasions. "You and I can take care of him."

On reflection, Cadi had to agree, she was right. Nevertheless, she welcomed Emery. Her help and support had been invaluable.

Fortunately, Ted managed to convince Stella to stay, assuring her that once he was fully recovered nurse Emery would leave. His death a few months later came as a huge shock.

With a weary sigh, Cadi rose to her feet and prepared for bed. Switching off the light she snuggled under the duvet. "Oh God," she said softly. "Thank you that Stella chose to stay. I know it's a long way for her to come, but I'm so grateful." Turning on her side she hugged her pillow. Exhaling softly, she closed her eyes.

Out in the hallway, Emery switched off the light. Opening her bedroom door she stood for a moment. Apart from moonlight filtering through the drapes, she was cloaked in darkness. Staring at Cadi's door, she tilted her head, her eyes narrowed as she listened. Hearing nothing, she entered her room and softly closed the door.

Chapter 3

Renee hummed to herself as she dropped her handbag on the passenger seat of the car. Her cases were packed, she was ready to go. Butterflies fluttered in her stomach, but she couldn't help grinning. At last after a successful exhibition, she had money in the bank, the house was locked up, and the open road beckoned.

Sliding into the driver's seat she started the engine. Her knuckles whitened as she gripped the steering wheel. Blowing out a few breaths, she dropped her shoulders and tried to relax. "Okay, it's a long way but I'll be fine. It's an adventure." She smiled as her tension eased. *It will be so good to spend some time with Cadi. I can't wait to see her.* However, as she put the car in gear, thoughts of her sister generated a feeling of unease.

She recalled her conversation with Cadi during the weeks of the exhibition. She sensed something was wrong…a strange weakness in her sister's voice, a noticeable breathlessness. It was obvious to Renee, Cadi's health was deteriorating.

Never before had she desperately wished for the closing day of an exhibition. Never before had she packed a case in such a hurry. Taking one last look at the house, she guided the car down the long drive and onto the main road. Glancing at the clock on the dash she breathed a sigh of relief. She wasn't a great one for greeting the dawn, but she needed to make an early start. The last thing she wanted was to be forced to negotiate strange country lanes in the dark. *Thank goodness for the Satnav*, she thought as she followed the instruments directions to the motorway.

The male voice was strangely comforting, but she knew better than to fully trust the device. Her lips flickered in a smile as she recalled a mishap a few months ago. She had followed its directions, and ended up outside a disused garage.

For backup, she had a map on the passenger seat, but it did little for her confidence, as she'd never been good at map reading. "Don't let me down Satnav," she said as the male voice directed her onto the motorway.

ক৯৯৯

Cadi opened her eyes as Stella entered the room with a breakfast tray. "How are you this morning my lovely?"

"My headache's gone, and I slept well," Cadi said struggling into a sitting position.

"Here, let me help you." Placing the tray on the end of the bed, she fluffed the pillows and helped Cadi to sit up.

"Thanks Stella."

"You're welcome, I'm glad you're feeling better." Lowering the legs of the tray, she placed it in front of Cadi. "I've made your favourite breakfast, scrambled eggs. Now eat it all," she said handing Cadi a napkin. "You need to keep your strength up. Your sister will be here later today." Stella chuckled at the beaming smile on Cadi's face. "That's better; you have some colour in your cheeks."

"I'm so excited Stella, I can't wait to see her. She's going to stay for a few months, isn't that brill."

Stella nodded. "Indeed it is. I'm glad she's coming. If anyone can get you on your feet, she can." Stella's knuckles whitened as she gripped her apron. Cadi's pale face, the dark shadows under her eyes, worried Stella. Her deterioration seemed so sudden.

With an inaudible sigh, Stella smoothed her crumpled apron and smiled at Cadi, pleased to see her

24

tucking into her eggs. "Ring the bell when you've finished, and I'll fetch the tray."

"Thanks Stella." Forking some egg, she paused. "Have you seen Emery this morning?"

Averting her gaze, Stella went to the window and opened the drapes. Warm sunshine streamed into the room. "What a lovely day, perfect for your sister's arrival." She walked to the door; pausing on the threshold she smiled at Cadi. "Why don't you have a nice hot shower, I'll be here if you need me."

"Thanks, but you haven't answered my question. Where is Emery?"

Stella rolled her eyes. "She's driven into town, so she'll be awhile. She said she's going to see the doctor and then the chemist."

Cadi lowered her fork, tilting her head, she stared at Stella. "I wonder why she's seeing the doctor. I know she needed the chemist."

"Could be she's running out of your medication, for all the good it does," Stella said.

"I know, but she's doing her best."

"I suppose so. Now you eat your breakfast. I'll come up later and check on you."

Cadi smiled and arched her brows. She was determined today of all days, there would be no negative talk about medication. Her sister was coming, and nothing and no one would be allowed to burst her happy bubble.

With a shake of her head, Stella left the room. Tutting to herself she plodded downstairs to the kitchen. Standing at the sink, up to her elbows in soap suds, she heard the nurse's car. Wiping her hands on her apron she went to the kitchen door. "You're back then," she said as Emery slammed the heavy front door.

"So it would appear," Emery said. Ignoring Stella she hung her coat by the door.

Stella opened her mouth to retort, but thought better of it. Shutting the kitchen door, she returned to the sink. Grabbing the frying pan, she attacked the egg stuck to it. Taking a deep breath, she rested her hands on the sink. *I need to stay calm. This is a special day for Cadi, and I mustn't spoil it.* Straightening her back, she grabbed a tea towel and dried the breakfast things. "All I need to do is stay away from her," she muttered. Just then the kitchen door swung open, and the nurse sauntered in carrying Cadi's breakfast tray. Stella grimaced. *Easier said than done*, she thought.

"Cadi will be down shortly," Emery said leaving the tray on the table. "She would like coffee in the library, if that's okay. Is the fire lit in there?"

"It is," Stella said, "I'll bring the coffee through." Taking the tray to the sink, she heard the door close. Chuntering to herself, she prepared the coffee and took it to the library.

Greeted by Cadi's warm smile and grateful, "thank you." Stella felt her irritation lift. Handing Cadi her coffee, she glanced round the room. "Where is—?"

"She's upstairs," Cadi said. Tilting her head she gazed at Stella. She could feel her tension. Taking her hand, she said softly, "You mustn't let Emery get to you."

"I try not to," Stella replied.

Cadi nodded. "I just wish you could both get on." Cadi sighed, deep down she knew Stella felt threatened by Emery. "I'm praying it will be easier when Renee arrives. I think a change of dynamics will make all the difference. Maybe we'll have a happy house again."

Seeing the sadness in Cadi's eyes, Stella squeezed her hand. "I hope so my lovely." Releasing her hand, she poured her another cup of coffee before leaving the room. Out in the hallway, she drew a tissue from her apron pocket and dabbed her eyes. Glancing up, she listened to nurse Emery's heavy footfalls as she moved around her bedroom. *I hope Cadi's right, she deserves some happiness.* Blowing her nose, Stella hurried to the kitchen.

❧❧❧

Holding the warm cup between her hands, Cadi gazed up at the painting. In the subdued light of a grey day, it appeared darker, akin to her mood. Sipping her coffee, she tried to shake off the feeling of melancholy. *My sister is coming, I should be happy.* "I am happy," she declared out loud.

Placing her cup on the table, she rose to her feet. Unsteady on her legs, she gripped the side of the armchair and studied the painting. Tilting her head she gazed at it. "I'm sure Renee painted the door closed." Moving away from the chair, she stared at it through narrowed eyes. *Strange, even from this angle it looks open.* Her trembling legs forced her to sit down. Resting a hand on her chest, she took a deep breath and glanced up. "I'm not imagining it, that door is slightly open. Maybe my eyes are playing tricks on me."

Lowering her head, she gently massaged her temples in an effort to ease the increasing pain in her head. Taking a calming breath, she closed her eyes and tried to relax. "I'll ask Renee about it, I could be wrong." Hearing a gentle tap on the door, she opened her eyes and sat up.

"Sorry to disturb you," Stella said closing the door quietly behind her.

"It's okay, did you want to take the tray? I have finished."

As Stella put the empty cup and carafe on the tray, she glanced at Cadi. "Are you feeling alright?"

Cadi shook her head. "I have a bit of a headache. Would you ask Emery to bring me some pain killers?"

"Of course I will. You seem to be suffering a lot of headaches lately."

Cadi nodded, she could see the concern in Stella's eyes. "Emery's medication doesn't seem to be working. Some days I feel worse than others." Sitting up in the chair, she gave Stella what she hoped was a reassuring smile. "Once I've had some pain killers I'll be fine." Glancing at her watch she felt a tingle of excitement. "Renee should arrive soon. I can't wait to see her."

Gently, Stella touched her arm. "I must say, I am pleased your sister is coming. Her presence will do you good."

Cadi leaned forward in her chair. "I'm so excited, Stella. I always feel good when I spend time with Renee."

Stella was pleased to see the spark of excitement in her eyes. "Maybe there will be some laughter again in this old house."

Cadi chuckled. "With Renee, that's guaranteed."

"That's good to hear. Now you rest while I go and find the nurse."

Closing her eyes, Cadi nodded. "Thank you," she said softly.

Entering the kitchen, Stella was surprised to see nurse Emery sitting at the table with a newspaper and a mug of coffee. "Cadi has a headache and needs some pain killers," she said. Without looking at the nurse she carried the tray to the sink.

"No problem, I'll go in a moment," Emery said glancing up.

Placing the tray brusquely on the draining board, Stella turned and glared at the nurse's back.

Sensing the housekeeper's hostility, Emery huffed and got to her feet. Pushing her chair back, she allowed it to scrape on the stone floor…something she knew irritated Stella. Striding across to a cupboard, she retrieved the tablets and hurried from the room, allowing the door to slam behind her.

Stella was about to shout, "What about a glass of water?" When she remembered, Cadi usually had a small bottle of water with her. Tutting, she rinsed out the coffee pot. Keeping busy helped her stay calm. Glancing towards the distant road, she prayed Renee would arrive soon.

I'm so relieved she's coming. Her presence will make all the difference to Cadi. A fleeting smile softened the tension on Stella's face. Nevertheless, comforting though the thought was, she struggled to shake off a feeling of disquiet.

৯৯৯

Clutching the tablets, nurse Emery stood outside the library door, listening. Apart from the clatter of pots in the kitchen, the house was quiet. Tapping on the library door, she didn't wait for a response, but strode in and handed Cadi the pills. "It's hardly surprising you have a headache," she said. "The noise that woman makes. If she's not banging pots about, she's singing all the time. I don't know how you stand it." Staring down at Cadi's pale pinched face, Emery frowned. "I can't understand why you need her. I could easily do what she does and in half the time."

Pausing, she smiled. "And with your sister coming to stay, I'm sure between us we could keep this place clean and tidy." Cadi's closed eyes and lack of response encouraged Emery. "You must agree, economically and in many other ways it's the most sensible solution."

Shifting in her chair, Cadi opened her eyes…grateful her headache had eased. "I agree, your suggestion is sensible, but I don't want my sister to come here and work. I want to spend time with her, and if I'm strong enough…to go out together. It would be good to get away from this house sometimes, to get some fresh air and a change of scene." Gazing up at Emery, she smiled. "You can understand that, can't you? Without Stella, it wouldn't be possible, but not only that, I like having her around." Squaring her shoulders, she added. "And personally, I enjoy her singing."

Hearing the firmness in Cadi's voice, Emery shrugged and turned away. "This is your home. You must do as you wish."

Cadi nodded. "Yes it is, and I will." Her brow furrowed as she watched the nurse plump cushions in the chair opposite. The woman's annoyance was obvious. Cadi reached out to her. "I appreciate everything you do for me, Emery. You didn't have to stay when Ted died, but you did, and I won't forget that. I don't know where I would be without you."

"It was my pleasure, I knew you needed me, and while that is still the case I will stay," she smiled. "However, I know someone who will be pleased to see me go."

Closing her eyes, Cadi sighed softly. "Take no notice of Stella. We're a good team, you, me and her. And with my sister arriving, everything will be perfect."

Hearing the tiredness in Cadi's voice, Emery moved beside her and placed a hand on her forehead.

Opening her eyes, Cadi murmured. "Your hand is lovely and cool."

"You do feel a little warm," Emery said. "Maybe you should go to your room and rest. After all, you want to feel strong and well when your sister arrives."

Cadi nodded. "You're right; I could do with a sleep, but only an hour or so. Please wake—"

"Don't worry, I will." Taking Cadi's arm, she helped her into the hallway, and onto the stair lift. "You go on up. I'll bring your medication and some lunch later." Standing at the bottom of the stairs, Emery rested a hand on the banister. Her lips pinched together, as she watched Cadi slowly ascend. Wiping her hands on her skirt, she returned to the library and closed the door.

Chapter 4

Renee's knuckles whitened as she gripped the steering wheel. She found herself glancing numerous times at the clock on the car's dashboard, and the petrol gauge. The gauge warned she was low on fuel, the clock warned, night was approaching. Both situations were beginning to worry her, but especially the thought of losing daylight and traveling in the dark. Not even the amazing sunset lowered her stress levels.

Going by her Satnav, she should reach her destination in a little over an hour. She felt sure she had enough petrol. Nevertheless, she found herself continually checking the fuel gauge. "On these country roads, garages are few and far between," she grumbled. Her stomach churned with the tension.

Due to a couple of refreshment breaks, and misunderstanding her Satnav's directions, the journey was taking longer than expected. She glanced at the countryside flashing past. Gone the green fields surrounded by hedgerows and woodlands. Now she drove through open moorland, peppered with stone walls and an occasional small village. Grey stone farms dotted the landscape. Hardy sheep grazed the rough pasture.

Taking a deep breath to ease her tension, Renee had to admit, bathed in the setting sun the landscape looked beautiful. *I wonder how close I am to Hadrian's Wall.* The Satnav's voice broke in on her thoughts. 'In two hundred yards, turn right,' it instructed. Glancing at a signpost, she saw the name of a village Cadi had mentioned and slowly smiled. She felt the tension in her shoulders ease. *Not far now, but I hope there's a garage around here somewhere.* The road she travelled widened, and as if in answer to her thought, a garage came into view. Peering over the steering wheel, she begged. "Please be open." With a sigh of relief she pulled onto the forecourt.

A large woman in grubby overalls waddled towards her. "You timed that right, pet. We were about to close. How much do you want?"

"Fill it up please," Renee said climbing out of the car to stretch her legs. "Do you know a place called Etal?" she asked.

"Oh yes, pet," the woman said as she led Renee to a small wooden building, and took her money. "But why would you want to go to there?" Shaking her head she stared at Renee. "There's nothing to see but a ruined castle." Raising a finger, she smiled. "However, the market town of Wooler is not far from Etal. It's a pleasant little town and has pretty much everything you need. "

"Thanks for the recommendation. But I'm going to stay with my sister," Renee explained. "She lives in the area of Etal, not far from the Scottish border."

"Ah yes, I know it well."

The woman's pout and slight shake of the head made Renee a little uneasy.

The woman noticed and was quick to reassure her. "There's nothing to worry about, pet. It's just not an area I visit much…too barren for me; nothing but rocks, heather and a few sheep." Smiling, she led Renee outside and locked her office door. "However, if you like walking you'll enjoy it. It's best avoided in the winter though."

"Why?" Renee asked.

"Oh, the winters up there are fierce! Snow so deep, the folks who live there can't leave their homes, and no one can reach them sometimes for weeks."

Renee smiled as she settled in the driver's seat, and wound the window down. "Well, thank goodness it's still summer."

The woman nodded. "Drive safely," she said. Waving her hand, she watched Renee turn onto the road and drive towards the village.

Renee glanced in her rear view mirror, the woman had gone. *Strange woman*, she thought. *Nice enough, but strange.* Shaking her head, she drove through the small hamlet, following her Satnav's directions, trusting it knew where she wanted to go. "Don't you get me lost," she growled at it. "Oops, I'm talking to an inanimate object." Chuckling to herself, she obeyed the Satnav and guided the car onto a narrow lane, which slowly morphed into a cart track. On either side of the road a forest of trees cast long shadows. Normally, such a place would make her uneasy and yet she felt relaxed. The petrol tank was full, and she had three quarters of an hour before darkness fell. Going by the Satnav, she should reach her destination in plenty of time.

ھ ھ ھ

Renee's first glimpse of Cadi's home, 'Five Acres,' took her breath away. The house nestled like an opulent jewel in the midst of an emerald setting. *Wow, why have I not been here before? It's certainly not for lack of an invitation.* She sighed. "Life is just too busy, and all this time Cadi has needed me." Swallowing the lump in her throat, she parked the car at the top of the long drive, rested her arms on the steering wheel and took in the panoramic view. In the distance, bathed in a beautiful orange and gold sunset, the grey stone mansion reflected the fiery hues of the sky. Renee could understand why Cadi loved the place and was loath to leave. "My home is lovely, but this is something else," she said softly.

The large mansion, surrounded by moorland and forest was like something from the set of a period drama. Renee could feel her imagination running wild. In her mind's eye she could see a handsome man mounted on a white horse galloping towards the house…her sister healthy and lovely standing in the doorway, waiting for him. Renee chuckled, *goodness woman, pull yourself together*! Nevertheless, the artistic potential of the surroundings made her heart flutter with excitement. *I'm so glad I brought my sketch pad and paints.*

Climbing out of the car, Renee stretched her arms to the sky. Breathing in the cool night air, she sighed with relief and smiled. "You got it right this time, Satnav." For a brief moment she stared at the house and surrounding grounds. *What a beautiful place.* However, the fading light, and the loud bark of a fox, brought her up with a start. Climbing back in the car she slowly negotiated the rough gravel drive.

"You have reached your destination," the Satnav informed her as she pulled up at the front door.

"Of course I have. Tell me something I don't know," Renee said with an amused smile. Getting out of the car, she went to the boot and retrieved her cases. *Crumbs, Cadi will think I'm never going to leave. Maybe I won't.* Glancing at the heavily carved front door and the large supporting pillars on either side, she almost expected a butler to appear, followed by numerous minions.

Dropping the heavy cases to the ground, she turned as the front door opened. The darkness receded as a warm welcome light spilled out.

Stella walked down the wide stone steps towards her. "Welcome, my dear, it is so lovely to meet you at last. Here let me take that," she said grabbing one of the cases.

"Really, it's alright I can manage," Renee said concerned the case would be too much for the older woman.

Stella chuckled. "I'm stronger than I look, pet" she said. "Come, let's get you indoors, you must be tired after your long drive."

"I am a bit, but the journey was good, and the countryside around here is awesome."

"It certainly is," Stella said, as she led Renee into the house.

Dropping her case on the floor, Renee's eyes widened as she stared around the spacious hallway. The interior of the house retained its elegant Georgian features. She ran her hand across a well-polished table, a vase of fresh flowers sat in the centre, their sweet scent permeating the space. A number of large oil paintings adorned the walls. Renee looked forward to taking a closer look at them.

Glancing up, she let her eyes follow the ornate winding staircase. But then she spotted the stair lift...an involuntary frown creased her brow.

Stella noticed. "It was put in for Ted," she said softly. "Cadi uses it, but not for long I'm sure. Soon she will be well, especially now you're here."

Renee gave a hesitant nod. "How is she? I can't wait to see her."

"She had a headache this morning, but I'm pleased to say, she improved as the day progressed. I think the thought of your arrival bucked her up. She's resting in the library at the moment." Stella gently touched Renee's arm. "I don't mean to put you under pressure, pet, it's just I know your presence here will be a huge tonic for her."

"I've come to help my sister," Renee said. "I want her to get well, and I will do my best to achieve that, no matter how long it takes." Stella's warm hug brought a smile to Renee's face. "It's lovely to meet you Stella," Renee said, returning the woman's hug. "You don't know how grateful I am, that you stayed with my sister. Both you and nurse Emery have been wonderful."

Stepping back, Stella stared into Renee's eyes, lowering her voice she said. "I would never leave her. I couldn't help her husband, but I will do everything within my power to help Cadi." Squaring her shoulders she smiled. "I know Cadi is eager to see you. If you follow me, I'll take you to her."

Renee could feel her stomach flutter as she followed the housekeeper.

As they approached the library door, Stella said, "I'm sure you would like some refreshment after your long journey. Would you prefer tea or coffee?"

"Tea would be lovely, thank you."

"Very well," Stella said. "Dinner will be ready in an hour."

"That's good. It gives me time to spend with Cadi."

Stella nodded, "Here we are pet." Opening the library door, she stood aside. "I will bring the tea in a moment," she said closing the door behind Renee.

Up on the landing hidden from view, Emery watched Stella and Renee chatting. Frowning, she pressed her lips together and leaned back against the wall. She could feel a hot flush rise up her neck. She knew Stella didn't like her, but she hoped she and Renee would become friends. "If they band together and try to get rid of me, they won't succeed," she whispered defiantly. Clenching her fists, she swung round and marched back to her room.

Having heard Stella tell Renee that dinner would be in an hour, Emery determined to join them. She planned to keep a strong presence in the house, whether Stella liked it or not. Walking across to her bedroom window, she stared out at the dark night. "I will not be leaving. This is where I belong." Thrusting her shoulders back, she left her room and strode down the hall to Cadi's. Switching on the bedside lamp, she stared around, her lips twitched in a slight smile as the soft glow illuminated the pretty room. Taking Cadi's pyjamas out of the wardrobe, she placed them on the pillow, before turning the bed down and checking the bathroom. *Right, time to get ready for dinner I think.*

Closing the bedroom door, she paused for a moment. Taking a deep breath, she squared her shoulders and strode down the hall to her own room.

ও৺ও৺

Renee paused by the library door, allowing her eyes to adjust to the soft lighting. "Cadi," she called. Hearing a soft murmur, she followed the sound. Cadi was curled up on the couch in front of a roaring fire. "Hello sleepy head," Renee said perching by her feet.

Opening her eyes, Cadi gazed at Renee. Half asleep, she couldn't be sure if it really was her sister, or an apparition. "Renee, is it you?" Pushing herself up, she reached out a hand.

Renee grasped it. "It's me Cadi. I arrived a few minutes ago. Squeezing her sister's hand, she studied her face...relieved to see a touch of pink on her cheeks. "How are you feeling?"

"Much better than I did this morning." She smiled. "Now you're here, I feel wonderful."

Moving closer, Renee embraced her. Biting her lip she drew back, her sister's fragility took her by surprise. Cadi's loose fitting jeans and baggy jumper concealed her weight loss. "Are you sure you're alright?"

"Don't worry, Renee, I'm fine, really." Raising a hand she touched her sister's cheek. "I have lost some weight, but now you're here, things will improve." Seeing the concern on Renee's face, she smiled. "I'm going to get well, and we are going to have fun, okay?"

The determined look in Cadi's eyes reassured Renee. "Okay," she said softly.

Hearing a light tap on the door, both sisters turned.

"I think that's Stella with tea," Renee said.

"Oh good, I'm ready for a cuppa."

"Me too, I'll let her in."

"Thank you pet," Stella said, as Renee closed the door behind her. Placing the tray on the coffee table, Stella asked. "Will you pour or shall I?"

"I'll do it," Renee said placing the pretty blue cups on their saucers.

Stella glanced at Cadi. "You look better my dear, there's some colour in your cheeks."

"I feel better, thanks Stella." Taking her tea from Renee, she smiled. "I'm so thrilled my sister is here."

"So am I," Stella said. With a knowing nod she went to the door. "I will call you when dinner is ready."

"Thank you," both girls chorused.

"She's so nice," Renee said.

Cadi nodded, "She is. I would be lost without her." Placing her cup on the tray, she sighed. "It's so good to have you here, Renee. I really do need you."

"I know you do and I won't be rushing to leave." Feeling a flush rise up her neck, she quickly added, "So long as that's okay with you, of course?"

"Are you kidding me? It's more than okay." She hugged Renee close, before rising unsteadily from the couch. "Come on, we'd best go to the kitchen. Stella will be calling us soon."

Renee supported her as they stepped into the hallway. Glancing up, she saw nurse Emery standing at the bottom of the stairs. "I've managed to get here," Renee said with a smile.

Cadi's voice rose with excitement as she wrapped her arms round her sister's waist, "I can't believe she is here. Isn't it wonderful?"

Emery nodded, "It certainly is. Welcome to Five Acres, Renee."

"Thank you, I'm glad to be here."

Cadi's happy voice urged them to hurry. "Come on, you two. Stella will be waiting to serve dinner." Linking arms they walked in a line towards the kitchen.

Hearing their giggles, Stella couldn't help but smile as she dished up the food. *I must admit, it's good to hear laughter in this house again. In this atmosphere Cadi will soon be well.* She was still deep in thought as they burst in and took their seats round the table.

Chapter 5

Renee finished unpacking and perched on the end of the bed. Dinner had passed in a blur of excitement. They all enjoyed the special meal Stella had prepared, and it pleased Renee to see Cadi eat well.

Kicking off her shoes, her thoughts turned to Emery and Stella. She liked them both, especially Stella. Emery, she decided would take longer to get to know.

However, tired after the long journey, her wish to retire early was not questioned and she was glad to escape to her room.

Cadi decided to join her as it had been a long and exhausting day. Seeing her sister forced to ride on the stair lift had brought a painful lump to Renee's throat. However, when Cadi showed her into the guest room, her spirit lifted. She couldn't help smiling as she stared around. The hint of pink on the walls gave the room a cosy feel. Pulled across, the dark pink drapes matched perfectly, adding to the warm ambience. Running her hand over the quilt she was sitting on, she fingered one of the tiny roses covering its surface. Even the pillows, and the soft fluffy towel folded beside her, were decorated with pink roses. Renee couldn't help admiring the handiwork.

Grabbing the towel she went into the spacious ensuite. The room was tiled from floor to ceiling in a muted pink, accentuated by an occasional large pink rose, which added a welcome splash of colour.

Apart from her concern over Cadi, Renee felt strangely peaceful. Sighing deeply, she prepared for bed. Slipping under the covers, she closed her eyes and prayed for Cadi, but sleep came quickly, the long journey had tired and stressed her.

It was still dark when she suddenly woke. Glancing at the clock on the bedside table, she saw it was three thirty. Grumbling, she rubbed her sleepy eyes…the time remained the same. Turning on her back she stared into the darkness. "What woke me?" She resisted the urge to switch on the bedside lamp. *If I do that, I'll never go back to sleep.*

Lying quietly, she listened to the sounds of the night. Raising her head, she heard soft pattering on her window and a loud whistling sound. Realising a storm was brewing, she let her head fall back on the pillow. However, as she lay there trying to get back to sleep, her ears pricked, she could hear footsteps and a creaking floorboard, as if someone were outside her door. Again, she felt the urge to switch on the lamp, but resisted. Sitting up in bed she listened, but all was quiet. *I wonder what that was.* Shaking her head, she snuggled under the covers. When she next woke it was six thirty. With a languid stretch, she sat up. Early rising was not her thing, but she knew further sleep would elude her.

Padding to the window, she pulled back the drapes and gasped. The view took her breath away. All around as far as the eye could see…moorland, festooned with heather and wild flowers, wet from the night's rain. The vegetation shimmered in the early morning light. In the far distance, rolling hills indicated the border of Scotland.

Hearing hoof beats, she glanced down. Below her window she could just see some buildings. Realising they were stables, her heart raced. "Cadi didn't say she had horses…awesome!"

Hurrying to the bathroom, she quickly showered and dressed. Ready to face the world she left her room. Closing the door, she paused for a moment in the hallway, the delicious smell of frying bacon and coffee wafted up the stairs. Her nose wrinkled in anticipation. Patting her stomach she hurried down the hall.

Passing her sister's room, she heard voices. Tapping on the door she poked her head in. Emery was sitting on the side of the bed holding a glass. "Good morning, is everything alright?"

Emery turned and smiled. "Yes, I'm just giving Cadi her medicine."

Cadi took the glass and sipped the cloudy liquid.

Emery grinned at her expression. "It's not that bad surely."

"It tastes horrible," Cadi said putting the glass on the bedside cabinet. "I'll finish the rest later." She turned to Renee. "Did you sleep well?"

Renee nodded, "I did, apart from hearing the storm at some point during the night, and a strange creaking outside my door."

"It's an old house," Emery said. "I hear all sorts of strange noises. You get used to it."

Cadi swung her feet to the floor and grabbed her robe. "Now that my sister is here, I can manage, thanks Emery. We'll see you at breakfast." She flashed the nurse a warm smile.

"Okay, don't be long. You know Stella likes to have meals on time."

The sisters grinned at each other as Emery left the room.

"Do you think she's a little peeved that I'm here?"

Cadi nodded, "Possibly, but she'll have to get used to it. Because I hope you'll be here a long time," Cadi said throwing her arms round her sister's neck.

Smiling, Renee returned her sister's embrace. If she could have read Cadi's thoughts, she would have heard, *like forever.*

Stepping away, Cadi took Renee's hand and led her to the cosy window seat. "It is so comforting, knowing you're next door. For the first time in ages, even with the storm, I slept well." Rubbing her chin, she gazed out of the window.

"What is it?" Renee asked.

"Nothing really, it just seems strange, that last night for the first time in ages, I had only the slightest nausea and no headache."

Renee frowned. "If this medication affects you like that, why doesn't she find something that suits you better?"

Shaking her head, Cadi pursed her lips. "Emery says this is the best that's available for my condition."

Sliding off the window seat, Renee clenched her fists. "What exactly is your condition?"

"To be honest, I'm not sure. I don't think Emery is either." Curling her legs beneath her she rested her head against the window pane.

Bathed in the soft light, Renee could see the translucency of her skin, the dark shadow under her eyes. "Have you seen a doctor?"

"Oh yes, a few months ago, I was really poorly and Emery sent for the doctor in Wooler. He wasn't my usual doctor, but he seemed nice enough. He gave me a thorough examination and took some blood samples." Running her hands through her hair she slipped to the floor. "The results were negative."

"That's good."

Cadi nodded. "It was a relief. The Doctor thinks my problem is something to do with my stomach and is organizing some sort of scan, but he warned me it can take ages for the appointment to come through, sometimes months."

Renee frowned. "I know, it's really annoying, the only way round it is to go private, but not everyone can afford that."

"I certainly can't," Cadi said as she padded to the bathroom. "I just hope I hear something soon. I'm going to take a quick shower, will you wait for me?"

"Of course, but don't be long I'm starving."

"Me too," Cadi said closing the bathroom door.

Perched on the window seat, Renee listened to the sound of running water. She had noticed how much stronger Cadi seemed when she walked to the bathroom. A sense of hope rose within her, while at the same time her head warned, caution. She struggled to understand why her sister appeared so laid back, almost as though she were unconcerned as to her condition. *How can you battle something, when you don't know what it is?* Renee clenched her fists, *sometimes ignorance is not bliss.* Pacing the room, she mulled over the various conditions she knew about, comparing them to Cadi's symptoms. The worst she blocked from her mind, tending to focus on those that were less serious.

Running a hand through her hair, she determined to have a serious talk with Cadi, pin her down, and somehow get a clearer picture of what was going on. *Maybe I should have a chat with Emery, she must have some idea what's going on, and she could speak to the Doctor and push for the scan.* The thought encouraged her. Nevertheless, Cadi's unquestioning trust in the nurse bothered her.

Renee let her mind wander back to childhood. She remembered how Cadi even as a youngster, had a thing about authority, bowing to anyone she deemed important, even when they weren't. Slumping on the window seat, she folded her arms across her chest, leaned against the window and sighed. It had annoyed her then, and it still did.

As a child, Cadi's angelic appearance, her sensitive nature drew Renee, and over the years their closeness increased. Being that much older, Renee had tended to mother her baby sister. However, now Cadi was a young woman, a widow, and Renee found her compliance to nurse Emery's wishes a little disturbing. *She needs to stand up for herself more. She's not forced to take the nurses medication, or for that matter keep her on.* Renee sighed. She knew her sister liked Emery. It was obvious they had become friends…Cadi trusted her. Renee knew how important that was. She remembered when their mother was really ill and how much she liked and trusted the nurse taking care of her. *But Cadi's young and has her whole life ahead of her.* The thought brought a flush to Renee's cheeks. She had no right to criticise or judge.

Hugging one of the cushions on the seat, Renee closed her eyes and prayed quietly. "Oh God, something is wrong here. Please help me. I need guidance." Opening her eyes, she stared out of the window. High in the sky storm clouds threatened, swallowing the distant hills. However, shafts of sunlight pierced the grey, defiant against the encroaching gloom.

Closing her eyes, Renee drew her legs up and hugged her knees. *Light will always pierce the darkness.* The thought brought a scripture to mind. 'My word is a lamp to your feet, and a light to your path.' *Thankyou Lord, I needed that.* Rubbing her eyes, she stood as Cadi emerged from the bathroom.

Tilting her head Cadi studied her sister. "Are you okay?"

Renee smiled and nodded. She was about to answer, when a loud gong echoed through the house.

"Oh goodness, that's our breakfast call. Please, Renee will you help me dress?"

"Of course, what do you need?"

Removing her robe, Cadi pointed to the wardrobe. "On the second shelf down you'll see a track suit that will do."

Lowering her head, Renee tried to hide her shock. Her sister had never been so thin. Dressed only in her underwear, she looked decidedly skeletal.

Seeing Renee's discomfort, Cadi gave her a reassuring smile. "I know I've lost a lot of weight, but don't worry it will come back on. I am determined to get well."

"I hope so," Renee said handing her the clothing. "I need to talk to you at some point soon."

"No problem. After breakfast we'll have coffee in the library. There is something I want to show you."

Seeing concern in her sister's eyes, Renee raised a brow.

"I'll show you later," Cadi insisted. "Come on let's get some breakfast before Stella has a hissy fit."

Arm in arm they walked to the stairs. Renee could feel Cadi's unsteadiness as she supported her and helped her onto the stair lift. Walking beside the slowly descending chair, Renee could feel a tightening in her chest. Even the delicious aromas wafting out of the kitchen did little to raise her spirit, in fact she felt slightly nauseous. She couldn't help wondering what her sister wanted to show her, and why she appeared anxious.

I guess I'll find out soon enough. Reaching the bottom of the stairs, she took Cadi's arm and together they walked into the kitchen.

"There you are," Stella said pulling out a chair for Cadi. "I was beginning to wonder if either of you wanted breakfast."

"Oh yes," Cadi said. "We're both starving." She glanced at Renee and grinned.

"That's good, you need to build your strength," she said patting Cadi's shoulder. Looking at Renee, she smiled. "Come on pet have a seat and I'll dish up."

Sitting beside Cadi, Renee glanced across the table at Emery.

The nurse peered at her over a glass of orange. "Is everything alright?"

Nodding politely, Renee poured herself and Cadi a glass. She couldn't help smiling at Stella's happy chatter and occasional humming. Sipping her drink, Renee felt a light touch on her arm, she glanced at Cadi.

"Welcome, to Five Acres," Cadi said raising her glass. "I hope you'll stay with us a long time."

"Thank you Cadi," Renee said touching her glass lightly against her sisters. Out of the corner of her eye, she saw nurse Emery raise her glass. "Yes welcome," she said.

"Thanks Emery." Renee glanced at Cadi. "I'm in no hurry to leave if that's alright with you?"

"Awesome," Cadi said with a delighted chuckle.

"Yes indeed," Stella said putting a plate of bacon and eggs in front of her.

Forking a piece of bacon, Renee glanced round the table. Smiling faces stared back at her. She felt at home.

Chapter 6

After breakfast, Renee and Cadi sat in the library in front of a roaring fire. Nurse Emery had just left after bringing Cadi her medication.

Leaning her head against the arm rest, Cadi closed her eyes.

"Are you alright?"

She shrugged. "I have a slight headache, but I'm okay."

Renee leaned forward in her chair and took a deep breath. She knew the subject she wished to broach was touchy, and Cadi's questioning stare did little to raise her confidence. Nevertheless, somehow she had to get to the bottom of what was going on. Coughing slightly to clear her voice, she asked, "Have you no idea what is wrong with you Cadi? I mean the doctor must have said something, given you an inkling." Frowning, she raised her hands. "How can he treat you, if he has no idea what is wrong with you."

Shaking her head, Cadi sighed. "Like I said earlier, he thinks it's a stomach problem, but doesn't know for sure. The last time I saw him, he reassured me that my condition isn't life threatening."

"How can he say that? If he's not sure what's wrong with you." Dragging her hands through her hair, Renee struggled to hide her frustration. "I think we should get a second opinion."

Shaking her head, Cadi curled up in her chair. "You're probably right, but I would rather wait for the scan."

"I don't mean to pressurise you, but—"

"Please, don't, Renee. I know you're trying to help, but I want to wait. I know things are moving slowly, but the appointment will come and the medication does seem to be working." Raising a hand she touched her face. "You must admit, I look better than I did when I came to your home."

Renee returned her sister's smile, but inside her stomach quivered. Having seen how thin she was… the sallow colour of her skin, no way could Renee agree. Nevertheless, noting her sister's relaxed posture and closed eyes she made no comment, although she determined not to wait too long before pushing again for a second opinion.

Leaving Cadi to rest a moment, Renee stood and wandered round the room. The night before she had been too tired to take it in, but now as she gazed around she understood why her sister loved it. Morning light streamed through the large picture window. Warmed by the fire the library felt cosy and welcoming. Every available wall space had shelving which reached from floor to ceiling, each shelf stacked with books. Glancing at a few titles, Renee could see, Ted had an eclectic taste in reading material. She noticed a set of first edition Dickens.

On another shelf were a number of titles by Tolstoy; two she knew well, War and Peace and Anna Karenina. However one was new to her, The Kingdom of God is Within You. Picking it off the shelf, she flicked through it. *When I have a moment, I will read this.* Putting the book back, she wandered across the room to another bookcase, allowing her eyes to wander over the numerous titles, most of which were thrillers by well-known authors. However, higher up, she noticed a couple of shelves filled with books on banking. With a frown and a shake of her head she moved away.

Running her fingers over the large desk, Renee walked around it and sat in the comfy swivel chair. Leaning back, she let her eyes rest on the painting hanging above the fireplace. It looked beautiful. The soft light in the room picked out the shadows, emphasising the gothic feel of the work.

"Can you see the door is open?"

"Ooh, you made me jump," Renee said.

"Sorry, but the painting is what I wanted to show you." Leaving the sofa she made her way to the desk.

"Come and sit here," Renee said, helping her sister into the chair. "What is it you want to show me?"

"Can't you see?" Cadi asked glancing up at her.

Resting her hands on the back of the chair Renee studied the painting. "What is it I'm supposed to see?"

Cadi sighed, "The door, its open."

Hearing the impatience in her sister's voice, Renee stared hard at the painting. But for the life of her, she couldn't see what Cadi meant. "What do you mean it's open?"

Rolling her eyes, Cadi asked. "Did you paint the door open or closed? I'm sure it was closed."

Walking round the desk, Renee stood closer to the painting, moving to look at it from different angles. Standing with her hands on her hips, she racked her brain. *She's made me think now. Did I paint it open or closed?* Chewing her lip, she tried to visualise herself painting it. "Closed," she said softly. Turning, she looked back at Cadi. "I painted the door closed."

"I thought so, but are you quite sure?" Cadi asked.

Seeing the confusion on her sister's face, Renee walked behind Cadi and placed her hands on her shoulders. Softly, she said. "I painted the door closed."

Reaching up, Cadi took Renee's hand and stared into her eyes. "Really, because it looks open to me."

Renee could hear the tremble in her voice. "I suppose because of the shading, if you look at it in varying light, it could look open." She stepped back as Cadi swung the chair round and faced her.

"The door has been open since Emery hung it on the wall."

Not sure how to respond to Cadi's determined expression, Renee shrugged her shoulders. "I can't see it, but maybe that's because it's my artwork, and in my mind I painted the door closed." Brushing a strand of hair away from her sister's face, she said softly. "Why is it so important?"

Rising to her feet, Cadi fixed Renee with a tearful gaze. "I'm not sure why." Turning her head she studied the painting and said softly, "I feel Ted is calling me to come through the door."

Renee could feel her throat constrict. She could hardly swallow never mind speak. Wrapping her arms round Cadi, she held her close. *Oh God is my sister going mad*. Her heart thudded in her chest.

Pulling away, Cadi stared at her. "Are you okay?"

Renee nodded. "I'm fine."

"You don't look it." Cadi took her hand and led her back to the warmth of the fire. "Sit down," she said patting an armchair. "I think we both need a cup of coffee, and I'll get Emery to bring me some headache pills." Grabbing a long silk cord she pulled it. Noting her sister's bemused look, Cadi smiled. "It rings a small bell in the kitchen. Ted had it installed before he became sick. He spent a lot of time in here, writing. He used to get frustrated when he needed refreshment and had to leave his work to find Stella." Leaning back in her chair, she closed her eyes. "I must admit, now that I suffer with ill health, I too find it extremely beneficial."

As they chatted, there was a soft tap on the door. "Can I get you something?" Wiping her hands on her apron, Stella hurried over to them. "Do you want coffee or would you prefer tea?"

"Coffee, please, Stella. And could you ask Emery to bring my pain killers, please?"

Tilting her head, Stella stared at her. "Are you alright, pet, you look a bit pale." She glanced at Renee. "In fact, you both do."

Renee smiled. "We're okay. Cadi has a headache that's all."

Stella frowned. "Nurse Emery is out. I believe she's driven into Wooler."

Cadi shook her head. "She's gone to town, again!"

"She left after breakfast." Stella pouted and shook her head. "She seemed in a bit of a mood as well. But don't you worry; I know where she keeps your headache pills." Striding from the room, she quietly closed the door.

Renee gently touched Cadi's arm. "I'm sorry if I contributed to your headache."

Cadi shook her head. "Don't be silly of course you didn't. I appreciate your concern over my health and if I don't hear about the scan soon, we will go for a second opinion. However, I wanted you to see the painting, I needed your reassurance. I couldn't remember if the door was closed or open." Glancing up at the painting, she pointed and said. "To me it looks open." Clutching Renee's hand, she whispered. "Am I going mad?"

Renee scooted closer and put an arm round her. "No, you are not going mad. Don't even think like that."

"How can I not? I don't understand what's happening to me." Tears trickled down her cheeks as she looked up at the painting. "To me the door is open, it's as clear as day."

Renee sighed. "I have no real answer, but it could be a side effect of the medication, or..." Pausing, she glanced at the small door in the far corner of the room.

Cadi followed her gaze, "What?"

"Subconsciously, it might have something to do with that door and what's behind it."

Taking a sharp breath, Cadi rose to her feet and stared at the door. Glancing at Renee, she said. "Do you really think so? Ted always kept it locked, and I have no idea where the key is."

"Have you ever been in there?"

Cadi frowned, "No, but one day when I came in here, Ted was locking the door. On reflection, he did seem agitated when he saw me."

"That seems strange," Renee said with a shake of her head.

"I thought so too. He was always so open and honest, not at all secretive."

"Well, he was obviously keeping something from you. Maybe we should try and find the key."

Hearing a knock on the door, Cadi sat down as Stella entered with a tray of coffee and biscuits. "Here we are," she said placing the tray on the side table. Taking a glass of water, she handed it to Cadi along with a couple of pills. "Take those and you'll soon feel better. Would you like me to pour the coffee?"

Cadi nodded, "Please, but before you do can I ask you something?"

Renee shot her sister a cautionary glance.

Cadi gave her a reassuring smile, as she asked Stella to look at the painting.

With her hands on her hips, Stella studied it. "I don't know much about art. But it looks good in this room and especially where you've hung it." Smiling, she glanced at Renee. "You're very talented, pet."

"Thank you," Renee said. "Look at it closely, and tell us if you think the door is open or closed."

Turning her head from side to side, Stella stared at the painting, squinting alarmingly.

Amused, Renee had to cover her mouth to stop herself from laughing.

Digging her sister in the ribs, Cadi frowned at her.

"Ouch!" Renee mouthed. Rubbing her ribs, she focused on Stella. "So, what do you think?" she asked, still attempting to hide her amusement at Stella's overly serious expression.

Muttering to herself, Stella continued to stare at the picture. Glancing at Renee and Cadi, she said softly, "To be honest I'm not sure. You see when I move it looks different." To emphasize the point, she swayed slightly. "In a certain light it could look open, but I really wouldn't swear to it." Facing them, she asked. "Why?"

Before Renee could answer, Cadi jumped in. "Because to me, Stella, it looks open."

Shrugging her shoulders, Stella joined them by the fire. "May I sit?"

"Of course," Cadi said pointing to the chair opposite. "Would you like a coffee?"

"No thank you," Stella said with a wave of her hand. "I'm concerned about what you are seeing in this painting." Pausing she lowered her head. Smoothing her apron across her knees, she made eye contact with Renee, before focussing on Cadi. Clearing her throat, she asked, "Do you think your medication is affecting you in some way?"

"I wouldn't be a bit surprised if it is," Renee said. "Maybe it highlights a fear. You do seem to have a thing about that door." She felt Cadi tense beside her.

Pursing her lips, Cadi sighed. "I don't know. Maybe you're both right." Twisting her fingers in her lap, Cadi stared at the door. "One thing I do know," she said firmly. "I need to find the key. Don't ask me why, I just know I must."

Renee and Stella stared at each other. They could see the concern in the other's eyes.

Resting her arms on her knees, Stella leaned towards Cadi. "I don't know what's in the room, pet. I've never been in there myself. However, I would imagine, knowing Master Ted as I did, it is probably full of important documents relating to his work as a banker." Sitting back in her chair, she wiped her hands on her apron and said softly. "If you want, while I'm cleaning around the house, especially in here, I will keep an eye out for the key."

"Oh, thank you Stella. I would be grateful. Going by the size of the lock in the door, I imagine the key will be pretty large and ornate, so it—"

"So it won't be easy to miss," Renee interjected with a chuckle. Winking at Stella, she said. "So, our mission, should we wish to accept it, is to find a large ornate key."

"In a nut shell, yes," Cadi said trying to smother her laughter. Raising her hands, she looked at Stella. "See what I mean."

"Indeed I do, pet. She brings laughter into this old house." Rising to her feet, she picked up the coffee tray. "I must organise lunch." Pausing in the doorway, she whispered. "Between us we will find the key."

As the door closed behind her, Cadi and Renee breathed a united sigh of relief. Renee noticed a rare expression of peace on her sister's face. Taking her hand, she asked. "Are you okay?"

Cadi smiled and squeezed her hand. "I feel better than I have for a long time. I know if we can find the key and get into that room, I will find the answer to my questions." Cupping Renee's hand in both of hers, she gazed into her sister's eyes. "Thank you Renee."

"What for?" Renee asked.

"For believing me and for taking my concerns about the painting seriously," she smiled. "You and Stella have made me realise, the door in the painting is not what this is about. It's about that door." Staring across the room, she said softly. "We need to get in there. I'm sure it's what Ted wants."

"We will, don't worry. If the key is in this house, we will find it." Gazing round at all the books, she said, "I have a hunch it's in this room, somewhere."

Cadi nodded. Closing her eyes, she leaned against the soft padding of the chair back. A cold shiver crept up her spine. She had a feeling they were getting close to something, but she had no idea what it might be. Only that it would affect them all.

Chapter 7

Sitting at the kitchen table, waiting for Stella to serve up a light lunch of ham and salad, Cadi noticed the housekeeper seemed quiet, thoughtful. Joining them at the table, Stella buttered some bread and drizzled olive oil over her lettuce leaves.

Tilting her head, Cadi watched her. This was a side to Stella she seldom saw. "Is something wrong?"

Halting her loaded fork mid-way to her mouth, the housekeeper shook her head. "No pet. It's just that since our talk in the library, I've been thinking."

"Ooh, that sounds painful."

"Renee!" Cadi's sharp tone brought an embarrassed flush to Renee's cheeks.

"Sorry, it slipped out." Looking across at Stella, Renee was relieved to see her smiling. "I apologise, Stella. It's my strange sense of humour. Please go on."

Putting her knife and fork down, Stella fixed them with a serious expression. The conspiratorial atmosphere was heavy in the room. "It could be nothing, but I feel I should mention it."

Both girls returned her gaze, their eyes never leaving her face.

"Tell us," Renee urged. She didn't realise how tightly she was gripping her knife. Feeling her hand cramp she released her grip.

Stella hunched her shoulders and instinctively lowered her voice. She told them how on numerous occasions, she had seen nurse Emery slip into the library when she thought no one was about. "Now why would she need to go in there, and in such a clandestine way?" Frowning she looked at Cadi. "She does it when you are upstairs resting, and when she thinks I'm out of the way in the kitchen."

Cadi smiled. "It's okay Stella. I'm sure it's not as clandestine as you think. Emery and I have discussed the door. Neither of us could figure out why it was always locked. She said she would try and find the key for me, but thank you for telling us."

Stella shrugged "Well I thought you ought to know. Her behaviour seemed a little strange."

Hearing the front door close, they all glanced up.

"Sounds like she's back," Stella said.

ೞೞೞ

Emery paused in the hallway. Tilting her head, she listened…all was quiet. Glancing at her watch, she frowned. *Its lunch time, where is everyone?* Unbuttoning her coat, she hung it on a hook by the door, before striding to the kitchen. "Anybody home," she shouted. Normally, the kitchen was the one room in the house guaranteed to be filled with noise. Whether animated chatter, the clatter of pots and pans, or the sound Emery most disliked, Stella's singing.

"In here," Cadi called.

Emery's lips twitched in a smile, as she opened the door. "So this is where you are. It was so quiet I thought you were all out." Breezing into the room, she made herself a coffee.

"Would you like some lunch?" Stella asked. "It's only salad."

"No thanks, I had something while I was out." Picking up her mug of steaming coffee, she glanced round at them. Seeing three pairs of eyes staring at her made her a little uneasy. "I'm taking this upstairs, if that's okay." Her eyes settled on Cadi, "You will need your medication soon. I'll bring it to you later."

Cadi nodded. "Okay, I'll be in the library."

Emery frowned at her. "Should you not be resting?"

"I will be, in the library."

Cadi's cheeky grin brought a smile to Emery's face. "Alright, I'll see you there later."

She has a nice smile. She should do it more often. Renee thought as she watched Emery leave the room.

෨෨෨

Stella sighed as she carried their plates to the sink. "She obviously hasn't found the key yet."

"No, she would have said if she had." Peering at them over her mug, Cadi whispered. "Do you think she knew we were talking about her?"

Renee frowned. "Why do you ask?"

She just seemed a little tense."

Renee shrugged. "I've no idea. You know her better than we do."

Cadi frowned as she sipped her coffee. For a moment they sat in silence, the only sound the loud tick of the kitchen clock.

Listening to the sound, Renee felt a cold chill run up her spine. Resting an elbow on the table she thoughtfully tapped her chin.

Cadi and Stella sat in silence watching her.

With a long sigh, Renee sat back in her chair. Looking at Cadi, she lowered her voice. "I know I want you to see another doctor, but in all honesty, I don't believe there is anything seriously wrong with you, other than normal grief over the loss of Ted. I wish

Emery would stop giving you this medicine, whatever it is."

Stella nodded in agreement. Taking Cadi's hand, she whispered. "Why don't you ask Emery what it is? Or better still ask her to make an appointment for you to see the Doctor."

"I agree, Stella," Renee said.

Cadi smiled reassuringly at them. "I will. I must admit I've noticed when I don't take her medication; I slowly begin to feel better. I have more of an appetite and less headaches. I've also noticed, Emery seems a little tense since you arrived Renee. I've no idea why."

"Maybe she feels threatened," Stella said.

"Why should she be? Nothing's changed as far as she is concerned."

Glancing at them both, she said. "Do you think she's worried, that when I'm better she'll have to leave?"

Renee and Stella glanced at each other. "Well, she will have to leave eventually, won't she?" Stella said.

Cadi shrugged. "I guess so."

Leaning across the table, Renee took Cadi's hand. "Initially, it will be hard for you to let her go, and I don't suppose she will be too happy about it. However, in the long run she will find another job, and more importantly you will be well and able to get on with your life."

"Cadi smiled. "That sounds good to me."

"Me too," Stella said. "You know I've always struggled with Emery. For some reason I don't fully trust her. Not even when she was looking after your husband. Don't ask me why, she's a nice enough person and she has been good to you."

Cadi nodded. "Yes, she has. I really appreciated her help with the funeral arrangements, and I can't tell you how relieved I was when she said she would stay. Just knowing someone else was in the house was a comfort to me."

Leaning across the table, Renee's brow knit in a frown. "Is there any way you can stop taking the medication?"

Cadi pursed her lips. "I suppose, and I could certainly ask her what it is. I know it's something for my stomach." Brushing a hand through her hair, she sighed. "When Ted died I really struggled with awful stomach cramps. It was so bad I had to go to bed."

Stella nodded. "I remember, and you were often sick as well."

Renee glanced at them both. "Were you taking the medicine at that time?"

Cadi shook her head. "No, when I first took it, it seemed to help. And when Emery said she would stay with me I felt a lot better, quite well in fact."

"Oh Cadi I wish I'd known. I would have come."

"I know you would. But at the time it wasn't necessary. I was okay. It's only recently that things have gone downhill." Staring at them both she smiled reassuringly. "I will talk to Emery about the medicine, but even more important, I want to find the key to the old door. I don't know why, I just know I have to get in there." Leaning back in her chair she chewed her lip. "So far Emery has had no luck finding it. Maybe we will have better luck." Frowning, she clenched her fists. "We must find it. The library is a big room. We will need to be methodical in our search."

Stella smiled. "Don't you worry, between us we can search that room a lot quicker than Emery, and I have an idea or two." Seeing the girl's optimistic expressions, she raised a finger and tapped the side of her nose. Rising from her chair she leaned on the table and fixed them with a determined gaze. "Trust me, we will find that key, and when we do we'll find the answer to all of this."

ନ୍ତ୍ର

A few days later, alone in the library, Renee stood by the desk tapping her fingers on the highly polished surface, she sighed. She had been searching for the missing key for almost an hour, with no luck.

Cadi's increasing frailty had galvanised her. However, lack of success and concern for Cadi, had taken the wind out of her sails somewhat. Over breakfast she had considered asking Emery to help in the search, but when she informed them she would be out for the day, Renee decided to search alone with a little help from Stella.

Gazing round the room, she tried to imagine where Ted would hide something like a key. "O God," she moaned. "Where is it?" A shaft of afternoon light highlighted a small cupboard in the far corner of the room. Particles of dust sparkled like miniscule diamonds in the sun's rays. With an inaudible breath, Renee hurried across the room and fell to her knees. "Please, please, let it be in here."

Pulling the doors open, she rooted through numerous documents and a heavy folder. There was no key. A small drawer under the lower shelf drew her attention. Her heart raced as she pulled it open. Squatting on the floor, she laid the drawer on the carpet beside her. She could hardly breathe as she stared at the contents. There were old cheque stubs, bank receipts, and a couple of ornate fountain pens.

However, her eyes were drawn to the numerous keys in the drawer. Most of them were modern, but there were a couple of old looking keys, one of which was quite large. Her hand shook as she reached for it. "Gosh, this was easier than I'd anticipated." Breathing a sigh of relief, she clutched the key and hurried across to the old door.

Standing in front of it, she stared at the ornate lock, and her heart fell…expectation melted away. She tried the key, but knew it wouldn't fit, it was too small. "Damn it! I should have known; that was way too easy."

Sighing with disappointment, Renee walked wearily back to the cupboard and returned the key to the drawer. Hearing Stella's voice out in the hall, she sauntered to the armchair by the fire and slumped into the softly padded cushion. Resting her head in her hands she stared into the fire. Hearing the library door open she raised her head. Stella's smiling face appeared round the door.

"Any luck?" She asked.

Renee groaned. "I thought I had." Pointing to the small cupboard she explained about the old key. "Sadly, it didn't fit. We'll just have to keep searching. It's got to be in here somewhere."

Stella nodded. "We mustn't give up, we'll find it." Going to the door, she paused. "I'm taking a cup of tea to Cadi, would you like one?"

"Yes, please. After the tea, I'll search again." As she waited for Stella to bring the tea she casually thumbed through a magazine which was lying on the seat, but there was too much going on in her head…her thoughts were everywhere.

Staring round the room, she scowled with frustration. "The key is in here somewhere I know it is. We will find it we have too." Raising her head she stared up at the ceiling. Her brow creased in a frown as an alarming thought crossed her mind. *Could Emery have already found the key?* "No," she said with a shake of her head. "If she had found it I'm sure she would have told us." Running her fingers through her hair, she sighed. "It's in this room I'm sure of it, but where?"

Chapter 8

The low growl of the car's engine echoed nurse Emery's mood. Her grey eyes darkened with aggravation. "It's alright for him. I'm the one doing all the dirty work. Scowling and grumbling to herself, Emery thumped the steering wheel as she guided the car down the long drive. Her heart raced as the house came into view.

"I need to find that damn key." Her lips pulled back in a snarl. After talking about it with Renee, she knew the others would be searching for it. These days she could only get in there at night, and searching with a torch wasn't easy, to say nothing of having to do it as quietly as possible so as not to disturb anyone. Almost worse than that was trying to negotiate the creaking floorboards outside the bedrooms, especially outside Renee's room. With an angry shake of her head, she wiped her sweaty hands on her coat.

Driving round the back of the house, she parked by the stables and got out of the car. Grabbing her handbag she paused and stared up at the house. A light shone from Cadi's bedroom window. She thought she saw the curtain move, but couldn't be sure.

Tutting to herself she pulled her jacket closer against the chill, and hurried to the back door. Closing it quietly she stood in the dark passageway, listening. Narrowing her eyes, she straightened her shoulders…fixed a friendly smile on her face and climbed the back stairs to her room.

ভ্রভ্রভ্র

Renee peeped through a fold in the closed drapes. "Emery is back," she said.

Cadi nodded. "I thought I heard the car. She always parks by the stables."

"Talking of stables; I didn't know you had horses."

Cadi smiled. She knew her sister loved to ride. "I was going to tell you, but with all that's going on I didn't get a chance."

"Believe me, I understand that, but one day if possible I would love to have a ride."

Cadi nodded. "You can ride any time you like. Emery rides most mornings. However, don't get too excited we only have Major; he's a sixteen hand hunter and Emery rides him. But there's old Berti he's an Irish cob. I'm sure she wouldn't mind if you joined her for a ride. She swears it gives her energy for the rest of the day. Major was Ted's horse. Before he became sick he used to ride out most mornings. Sometimes, I would join him on Berti." Sighing, she leaned against the headboard. "I miss those times. I miss him."

Renee perched on the side of the bed and took her hand. "I know you do. I wish I could do more to help. We need to get to the bottom of what's going on here, and fast." She gently squeezed Cadi's hand it felt cold. Renee knew Cadi was keeping up a brave front, anyone with eyes in their head could see she was unwell. "How are you feeling?" She asked gently. "Be honest with me."

Cadi pouted and shook her head. "It's difficult to explain. My head hurts most of the time, and I constantly feel nauseous and so tired." Raising her hands she showed them to Renee. "Look at my nails and fingers they're so red." Closing her eyes she rested her head on the pillow and sighed. "But the worst thing is not being able to sleep."

Leaving the bed, Renee paced the floor. "When did this start?"

"Not long after you arrived."

Pursing her lips, Renee nodded. "I really don't understand it. I thought my being here would be good for you. But you appear to be getting worse not better."

Sitting on the edge of the bed, Cadi ran shaky hands through her hair. "I know it's weird. I'm so happy that you're here, but at the same time disappointed that my health is not improving."

Joining her, Renee put an arm round her shoulders. "Don't you worry we'll get to the bottom of it. Stella and I are going into Wooler tomorrow. She will show me where the surgery is. I've already made an appointment to speak to your Doctor. I want to know what medication he's giving you and how close you are to having this scan."

Raising her head, Cadi stared at her sister.

Renee could see the concern in her eyes. "Try not to worry, Cadi. Stella and I will find out what's happening." Pulling Cadi closer she added firmly. "And trust me, we will find the missing key."

"I hope so," Cadi said softly.

The sound of the dinner gong reverberated through the house, the noise echoing their sombre mood.

Renee took Cadi by the arm. "It sounds like dinner's ready. Come on, let's go and eat."

"I'm really not hungry," Cadi said pulling back slightly.

"I know, but you need to keep your strength up, and you know how Emery fusses. You don't want to give her any excuse to bully you, even though she means well."

Cadi huffed and nodded. "You're right, she does go on sometimes."

Smiling, Renee gently pulled her to her feet. "Trust me Cadi you'll come through this." Renee tried to ignore the slight tightness in her chest as she guided Cadi along the passage and settled her on the stair lift.

Before she pressed the button, Cadi reached for Renee's hand. "I'm so glad you are here."

Renee gently squeezed her hand. So am I. Following the stair lift as it slowly descended, she glanced at the large portrait of Ted. His dark eyes appeared to return her gaze. "And I'm in no hurry to leave," she said softly.

Chapter 9

Renee linked her arm through Stella's, as they made their way along Wooler's main road. Shoppers thronged the street, forcing them at times to walk single file. It was market day and the small town was busy.

The warm sun and fresh air raised Renee's spirits. Hope fluttered like a butterfly in her stomach. "This is a nice little town," she said as they made their way towards a small café.

"Ai pet, it is."

"Is your house nearby?" Renee asked.

"It is. I've lived in this town all my life."

"So you must know pretty much everyone."

Stella nodded. Pausing outside the café, she opened the door. "Here we are. You find a table and I'll order the drinks."

Renee settled at a table by the window. She loved to people watch, but today there were important things to discuss. Her heart raced uncomfortably as she thought of Cadi alone in the house. Realising she was nervously twisting the paper napkin she dropped her hands into her lap.

Stella returned to the table and sat across from her. She noticed Renee's anxious glance through the window, the unconscious frown on her face. "It's alright," she said softly. "Cadi will be fine."

"I know I just don't like to leave her on her own."

"She's not alone. I asked James, Bob's son to remain in the house and keep an eye on things, and Emery assured me she was only going for a short ride."

Renee sighed with relief. "That's good."

"She'll be quite safe with James in the house. If she needs him she only has to ring the bell. James's father Bob had been with Ted for more years than I care to number. Young James is a new addition to the staff." Seeing the concern in Renee's eyes, she reached across the table and touched her hand. "Relax pet. I've known the family for years. They can be trusted."

Renee nodded. She was about to speak, but noticed the waitress making her way to their table.

Placing steaming mugs of coffee in front of them, the young woman asked. "Can I get you anything else?"

"No thank you," Stella said with a shake of her head.

Sipping her coffee, Renee felt the strong hot liquid sooth her tangled nerves. Glancing at Stella over her mug, she whispered. "Cadi seems to be improving."

Stella nodded. "I'm doing my best, keeping her on a simple diet seems to have helped. It was awful seeing her sick all the time."

Renee nodded, "Yes, it is. She throws most of the medication down the sink when she can."

Stella sighed, "I hope she is doing the right thing. If she does have a stomach problem she could need the medicine. Not that it seems to help her much. She's been taking it for a long time and is really no better."

"That's true. I'll be glad when she can have the scan. We need to know what's going on."

Lowering her head, Stella stared into her mug. "Exactly, and we need to find out soon."

Reaching across the table, Renee gently touched her hand. "Thank you for showing me the surgery. Now I know where it is it will be easier when I go to see him. I can't believe it's taking this long to get a scan."

Stella nodded. "I can't say I liked him much. I felt his bedside manner left a lot to be desired." Her hands trembled as she held her mug. "And there was something about his familiarity with Nurse Emery that bothered me."

"How do you mean?" Renee asked.

Stella shrugged. "I can't explain it. I just felt they knew each other." Pausing she took a sip of her coffee. Peering at Renee over her mug she said. "I watched from the kitchen as Emery showed him to the front door. Their behaviour was clandestine with a lot of whispering, which I don't think is normal between a doctor and a nurse."

Renee chewed her lip as she gazed through the café window.

Watching her, Stella said. "Don't worry. It may just be me. I do have a vivid imagination."

Renee shook her head. "I hope that's all it is." Gazing at Stella she asked softly. "Do you know where Ted is buried?" Stella's sharp intake of breath did little to reassure her. "He was cremated, wasn't he?"

"Oh Renee, Please don't talk to Cadi about it. Ted's instructions were that he wanted to be buried. There's a crypt in the grounds of the house. Both Ted's father and mother are in there. He told Cadi. In fact I believe it's written down somewhere, but no one could find it. He told her if anything happened to him, his last wish was to join them. As it is, all that's in there are his ashes in a large urn."

"Poor Cadi, I should have been here. I feel awful about it."

Stella shook her head. "It's not your fault. You were hundreds miles away at the time. I did my best, but there was so much to organize I didn't know where to start first. Thank goodness nurse Emery took over and organised everything. Cadi was naturally in shock…grief stricken. She was alone and with no one to help or advise her, she just lost control of the whole situation. It pretty much pushed her over the edge."

Renee sighed. "Do you know if Ted has any relatives?"

"Not as far as I know. Surely if there were, they would have come forward by now. When the solicitor read the will, it was clear, Ted left everything to Cadi."

"But what would happen if God forbid something should happen to her?"

Stella shrugged. "I have no idea. I suppose the solicitors would have to search for a relative."

Renee frowned. "I'm sorry to talk like this Stella. It's just something that occurred to me."

"Maybe you need to talk to her about it. Ask her if she has made a will. If not maybe she should."

"I'm not sure I can, at the moment it would be insensitive of me. I know how I would feel. It would be like telling her to put her house in order. I can't do it, maybe when she is better."

Stella nodded in agreement.

"I'll tell you one thing though," Renee said. Leaning closer she lowered her voice. "I want to find out what it is that Emery is giving her, and I'm determined to find that key. If we can get into that small room in the library, I believe we'll find the answers we're looking for."

Stella nodded. "I'll help you in any way I can. Between us we'll find it." Looking at her wrist watch she got to her feet. "We need to go."

Grabbing their coats they left the café and hurried back to the car. Lost in their own thoughts, they drove home in silence.

Steering the car down the long drive towards the house, Renee saw Emery riding across the field towards the stables. She nudged Stella. "There she is. It looks like she's been out longer than she said."

"I suppose she thought with James in the house, Cadi would be okay."

"That's not the point though, is it? James shouldn't have that responsibility."

Stella shrugged, "True, but I'm not going to tell her."

Renee glanced at her. "Coward," she said with a smile.

Stella grinned at her.

Renee parked the car and unloaded their shopping. "I'll leave you to put things away while I go and check on Cadi." As Renee hurried across the large hallway towards the library she spotted James sitting by the fire.

He rose to his feet as she approached. His blues eyes twinkled as he responded to her smile. Retrieving his cap from the arm of the chair he clutched it nervously. "Everything is okay miss," he said with a bob of his head.

"Thank you James. I know asking you to do this took you away from your work, but I do appreciate it."

"It's a pleasure miss," James said. "My father and I are happy to help in any way we can."

Gazing into his blue eyes, Renee felt a strange lightness in her chest. Taking an inaudible breath, she tried to cover her embarrassment. "Nurse Emery has returned from her ride, so it's okay for you to go now. I imagine your father will need help with Major."

"Yes he will, thank you miss." Running a hand through his blond hair he put on his cap, smiled and walked away.

Watching him go, Renee felt a flush of heat on her cheeks. Embarrassed, she shook her head. "Pull yourself together woman," she muttered as she opened the library door. Seeing Cadi curled up on the settee, she smiled. Fresh logs crackled and hissed on the fire. The pleasant smell permeated the room. "Are you alright? We tried not to be too long."

"I'm fine." Raising her hand she pointed to the fireplace. "As you can see James refreshed the fire and sat with me for a bit." She glanced towards the door. "Is Emery back?"

Renee nodded. "She was riding across the field towards the stables when we got home."

Taking Renee's hand, Cadi pulled her closer. Snuggling into the corner of the settee she gazed at her.

Seeing the amused twinkle in her sister's eyes, Renee frowned. "What?"

"You've met James haven't you?" Cadi chuckled at her sister's discomfort. "Sorry, I don't mean to embarrass you, but—"

"Yes, okay," Renee quickly interjected. "He's very nice." Lowering her head she hoped her long thick hair would hide the redness of her cheeks. Raising her eyes she scowled at Cadi.

Laughing, Cadi raised her hands. "Oh alright, point taken, enough about James." Leaning towards Renee her expression darkened. "Did you manage to find out anything?"

"Not really. Stella showed me where the surgery is, so at least now I know where to go. I'm keen to have a word with your Doctor."

"That shouldn't be a problem."

Renee nodded, "I hope not. I'd like to know what this medicine is you're taking."

"Me too," Cadi said. "As you're my sister you should be able to find out."

"Don't say anything to Emery for the moment. I don't want her to think I don't trust her. It's just that asking her would be more difficult than going to see the Doctor. For the moment we all have to live with Emery, and I don't want your care affected by any negative response from her." She glanced at Cadi. "And I know you are fond of her, so I don't want to upset her."

"I won't say anything, but what about Stella?"

"Don't worry about Stella, she won't say anything."

A slight frown darkened Cadi's eyes.

Tilting her head, Renee stared at her. "What?"

"Nothing really, but I know Stella struggles with Emery, she always has. She feels Emery breezed in and took over. Stella had been with Ted a good many years and I think for a while she felt Ted didn't need her anymore. It all got extremely tense and upsetting. Ted managed to sort it out, but it was obvious to me Stella and Emery were never going to get on."

Renee sighed as she stared into her sister's troubled face. "It's been a hard time for you, hasn't it?"

Cadi nodded. Looking away she wiped the tears from her eyes. "I really loved Ted and I miss him so much."

Renee held her hand. "Of course you do. I'm so sorry I couldn't come to the funeral. If I had, you would have no need of Emery."

"Please don't think like that. You are here now, and even though I don't have a faith as strong as yours, I have never believed in coincidence. I believe things happen for a reason." Cadi squeezed her sister's hand. "I'm going to get well, and we are going to find that hidden key." She glanced towards the small door and smiled.

Her sister's positive words brought tears to Renee's eyes. She felt a pleasant fluttering in her stomach as she looked round the room. *We will find the key and I pray it will be soon.*

Chapter 10

A week had passed and the tension in Five Acres was palpable. Renee could only watch as her sister struggled with the usual good days and bad days. Not being able to find the missing key added to her stress. Rooting through numerous dusty books and coming up empty every time was beyond distressing. She had hoped Emery would have more luck, but she hadn't found the key either.

This particular morning, Renee had an appointment with Cadi's Doctor. She felt nervous but hoped the meeting would prove fruitful. Keeping it a secret from Emery had not been easy. She had no desire to upset the nurse and felt bad about going over her head.

"Cadi is your sister," Stella said at breakfast. "You have a right to a second opinion." She watched Renee play with her bowl of cereal. "What time's the appointment?"

Renee looked at her watch. "In an hour, so I'd better get a move on."

Stella nodded. "Don't let him bully you. Stand your ground and find out as much as you can."

"Oh I will, don't worry. I had enough of a job getting the appointment I'm not going to waste it."

Stella sighed. "Getting to see a Doctor these days is almost impossible. It's ridiculous!"

Renee nodded. "What time did Emery leave?"

Stella glanced at the clock on the wall. "I would say about half an hour ago."

"Okay, I'm going I'll see you later."

"Drive carefully and good luck."

"Thanks," Renee said as she hurried into the hall and grabbed her coat off the hook. Opening the front door she was greeted by a blast of frosty air. For a second it took her breath away. Standing on the steps for a moment she took in the view. All around the landscape sparkled with a dusting of frost. She couldn't help smiling. *It's so beautiful here.* Searching in her bag she found the car keys, as usual they were hiding at the bottom.

Climbing into the car she was grateful to escape the chill wind. The tyres crunched pleasantly on the gravel as she drove the car towards the main gates. Once on the main road she increased her speed. "I can't afford to be late," she muttered.

She arrived at the surgery in plenty of time and found a secluded spot to park. Looking at her watch she saw she had a good fifteen minutes to spare and decided to sit in the car. Resting her arms on the steering wheel she watched patients arrive and leave. She was about to get out of the car when she saw Emery leaving the surgery with a man. They stood together at the main entrance, and to Renee's surprise the man leaned over and kissed the nurse.

Renee gasped and slid down in the seat. Peering over the steering wheel she watched Emery stride to her car and the man head back inside the building. Once Emery had driven away Renee snatched her bag off the back seat and hurried into the building. For a moment she stood in the entrance, she needed to calm herself, her mind was buzzing with questions. *Who was the man with Emery? She had never mentioned there was a man in her life.* Renee frowned and shook her head. *But then, come to think of it none of us know much about her private life.*

Standing by the door deep in thought the receptionist's voice took her by surprise.

"Can I help you?"

"Yes, I have an appointment with Doctor Mason." She gave the receptionist her name.

"That's fine. Please take a seat the Doctor will see you in a moment."

Renee hesitated.

"Is there something else?" the woman asked.

"I was wondering if nurse Emery is attached to this surgery."

The receptionist smiled. "Oh yes, Emery is married to Doctor Mason. They've not been here that long. Do you know her?"

Renee smiled and nodded. Taking a seat she waited to be called. *Now I know why Stella thought the Doctor and Emery's behaviour at the house was strange.* Renee chewed her lip as she sat waiting. *This is all a little awkward, but now I know why Emery keeps coming into town.*

Hearing a buzzer she glanced up at a moving notice board. Her name was called. Taking a deep breath, she left her seat and followed the long hallway to room five. Tapping on the door she walked in. "Good morning," she said softly.

The man sitting at the desk looked away from the screen in front of him and smiled at her. "Good morning. I'm Doctor Mason, what can I do for you?"

For a brief moment Renee stood there looking at him. Even seated she could see he was tall and well built. With his neatly trimmed facial hair and good looks he wasn't your average Doctor...not what Renee had expected anyway. *Well done Emery*, she thought. A little flustered she sat in the proffered seat.

"So, how can I help you Miss—?"

"Renee Reid. Actually, I'm here on behalf of my sister, Mrs Cadi Grey."

"I see. Let me take a look."

Before he typed on his keyboard, Renee thought she saw a flicker of recognition in his eyes. She noticed his brow wrinkle in a dark frown as he brought up Cadi's notes.

Keeping his eyes on the screen, he said firmly. "I can't discuss one of my patients with you, Miss Reid."

"Oh I think you can. As I said I am her sister her only relative. I need to know what's wrong with her, what her medication is for and when will she have the promised scan?"

He swung his chair round to face her. "That's a lot of questions. As far as the scan goes I have no answer, but I can ring the hospital and try to chivvy them up. As to what is wrong with her, I don't believe it is anything serious. She has a chronic stomach problem. She told me she had issues from childhood."

What he said was true, so all Renee could do was nod. "But what about the medication nurse Emery is giving her?"

At the mention of Emery she noticed the slight smile at the corners of his mouth. Renee cringed. Something about him unnerved her. Not only that, there was something about his face. He reminded her of someone, but she couldn't put her finger on it.

He made no mention of Emery as he explained about the medication. "At the moment I have her on Cholestyramine. It should be helping her condition."

Renee shook her head. "It isn't, in fact I feel she is getting worse. I would like her to have this scan as soon as possible."

"Well as I said, I will do my best to move things along. However, there is a long waiting list and the most serious cases are seen first, and Mrs Grey is not serious. So I would encourage you not to worry. Let her have plenty of rest and keep her fluid content up. I'm sure nurse Emery knows what she is doing."

Again Renee saw the unpleasant flicker of a smile…a smile that didn't make it to his eyes. Raising a hand he pointed to the door. "If that's all I can do for you, I'm afraid I have other patients to see." His dismissive tone ended the appointment.

Staring him in the face, Renee got to her feet and left the room. Hurrying out of the surgery hot tears stung her eyes. Anger rose like bile in her throat. Slumped in the driver's seat she beat the steering wheel with fisted hands. Her tears flowed freely. Grabbing a tissue from her bag she blew her nose and took a few calming breaths. *He's lying, I know he is.* Leaning against the head rest she waited until she felt calm enough to drive.

৯৯৯৯

Dr Mason left his chair and peered discreetly through his blinds. He could see her sitting in the car. She was clearly upset. Grinning, he returned to his desk and picked up the phone, lounging in his chair he waited. The voice on the other end sounded harassed.

"I've had a visit from the sister. She's not going to be a pushover. You're going to have to be careful. But at the same time hurry things up." His lips formed a tight line as he listened. "I know you're doing your best, but I don't want her getting suspicious." Frowning, he pulled the phone away from his ear. "Stop shouting, just get this sorted and soon."

83

Growling, he slammed the receiver down. Closing his eyes for a moment he breathed deeply before calling in his next patient.

৵৵৵

Struggling to control her tears, Renee clung to Stella. How she got home, she had no idea. She'd driven in a daze. Reaching the house, she rushed to the kitchen, saw Stella and burst into tears.

"Come on pet sit down. Have a cup of tea and tell me what happened."

"I don't know where to start Stella, he was horrible. There was something about him. He reminds me of someone but I can't think who." Resting her chin in her hands she watched Stella make tea.

"Here you are get this down you." Reaching across the table she patted Renee's hand. "Right, now tell me what they are doing about Cadi."

Renee sipped the hot tea, it calmed her…helped her collect her thoughts. "He said Cadi has a chronic stomach problem, but that it's not serious. He told me what medication she is having and for the moment all she needs is rest and plenty of fluids."

Stella frowned. "Okay, that all sounds reasonable so far, but what about the scan?"

"He said the scan will take some time to arrange as they are seeing serious patients first, and my sister is not considered serious." Clenching her fists Renee banged the table. "Who's he kidding? He should come and see her."

For a moment they sat in silence digesting all the information. Renee finished her tea and put the mug down. "You know Stella," her voice dropped to a whisper. "I'm beginning to think you could be right about Emery." Seeing Stella's arched brows she continued. "Emery is married to this Doctor Mason, not only that I saw them kissing outside the surgery." She paused as Stella gasped.

"You're kidding me?"

"No it's true. She is married to the Doctor, the receptionist told me. That's why they behaved the way they did when he came here to visit Cadi. You were right to be suspicious. I don't know what's going on but Emery is definitely involved, and I'm beginning to fear for my sister. I'm so grateful you can stay with us and so is Cadi. I know she is comforted having you here." Staring into Stella's eyes, Renee could see a cloud of concern. "What is it?"

"I'm happy to be here, but I worry Emery is wondering why I've moved in."

Renee shook her head. "Stop worrying about Emery. I'm sure she is not bothered one way or another. The dining room needs decorating and you are the housekeeper. It's your job to organise everything, and to do that you need to be here."

Stella lips flickered in a smile. "I suppose you're right."

"Of course I am."

They heard the front door slam and sat in silence. They could hear the sound of heavy footfalls coming towards the kitchen.

"It doesn't sound like Emery," Renee said rising from her chair.

Stella nodded and indicated she should sit down. "It's okay it's James. He said he would pop in and take some measurements in the dining room."

Renee breathed a sigh of relief as James popped his head round the door.

"Is there any coffee going?" He asked with a cheeky grin.

Stella filled a large mug and handed it to him.

"Thanks, I'll take this with me."

"Have you seen Emery?" Renee asked.

James nodded. "She's gone out on Major. I imagine she'll be back in about an hour." Scowling he held his mug between his hands. "I wouldn't mind, but sometimes she brings the horse back in a right old lather."

Renee glanced at Stella.

"Go, search while you have the opportunity," Stella said with a flick of her hand. "I'll see to Cadi and keep an eye out for Emery."

Renee smiled at James's creased brow. "We have to take every opportunity to search the library for a missing key. You haven't by any chance seen an old key lying about?"

James shook his head, "Sorry I haven't. But I'm happy to help you search for it. I can spare half an hour." Renee's enthusiastic response brought a smile to his face.

Lowering her head Renee blushed. She loved the way his blue eyes crinkled when he smiled. *Pull yourself together woman*, she silently chided. Seeing Stella watching them, her arms folded across her chest and a knowing expression on her face, Renee scowled playfully at her.

"Come on then James," she said, in a voice as matter of fact as possible.

Stella chuckled to herself as she washed a few pots and prepared some lunch.

ৎৎৎ

Apart from the frustration of not finding the key, Renee had grown to love the library. It smelt of old books... of well used leather chairs, and at times she was sure she could detect the delicate aroma of Ted's pipe tobacco. She found that a little unnerving and chose not to say anything to Cadi.

Renee found James presence comforting as they stood together gazing round. A log fire blazed in the hearth. Warm sunshine streamed through the window...flecks of dust danced in the rays.

Shrugging her shoulders she glanced at James. "Where do you want to begin?" Making a wide sweep with her hand, she said. "I've had most of the books off the shelves, so there's not much point looking there."

James nodded in agreement. "I'll start looking round by the fire." Glancing at the old rugs covering the floor, he asked. "Have you tested any of the floorboards?"

Renee felt a fluttering in her stomach. Looking up at him she smiled. "That's a brilliant idea. Some of the floorboards do creak." Itching to get going she walked slowly towards the desk, while James began his search round by the fireplace.

Renee was about to lift another rug when James called her over. Grunting, she got up off her knees. She could see him tapping the brick fire surround.

"Some of these are loose," he said.

Hurrying over Renee could see the excitement in his eyes.

"It may be nothing," James said. "But I think we should take a look." One of the bricks he was wiggling came away easily in his hand. Stooping down he peered into the small cavity. "Nothing in there," he said.

Replacing the brick he looked at Renee. "There are plenty of loose ones so we need to keep looking."

Renee glanced at her watch, time had flown. Her heart sank at the thought. Emery could already be back from her ride. Renee no longer felt she could fully trust the nurse. *I don't want her searching for the key. I need to find it and fast.* Initially, she couldn't understand Stella's dislike of the woman, but slowly her discernment was proving to be right.

Seeing her concerned expression, James nodded. "You're right we'd best stop." Placing a gentle hand on her shoulder, he whispered. "This is where you need to look when you next have a chance."

Rubbing her hands together Renee stared at the fire surround. A strange anticipation made her whole body tingle. "You could be onto something here," she said softly.

"I know, but keep it—"

A tap on the door stopped him in mid-sentence. Moving away from the fireplace, they both smiled as Stella poked her head round the door. Entering the room she closed the door softly behind her. "I just wanted to let you know. Emery is back. She's gone up to her room." Looking at her watch she told them lunch will be ready in ten minutes.

James strode to the door. "Thanks Stella I'll go and help dad with Major."

"You're welcome to have some lunch with us," Stella said.

"No, thank you. My dad will need some help and we've brought sandwiches." Smiling at Renee, he said. "See you soon."

"Yes, and thanks for your help."

"You're welcome. I hope the hunt for the key is successful." Giving her a wink he turned and strode from the room.

Stella couldn't help smiling at the pink glow on Renee's cheeks.

Renee scowled at her.

"What?" Stella said with a grin.

"You know jolly well what!"

"He's a really nice young man and he seems to like you."

"Maybe he is and maybe he does. However, we have a serious situation and that's all I can think about at the moment."

Stella nodded, "You're right."

Renee smiled and took her arm. "Maybe if things were different, who knows?"

Leaving the library they slipped unnoticed into the kitchen. The welcome smell of chicken soup greeted them.

Renee placed a couple of bowls and spoons on a tray. "I'll take some up to Cadi and see if I can get her to eat."

"Good idea." Stella buttered some bread. "Tell her I'll bring her a cup of tea later. You'd best take these just in case," she said putting two pain killers on the tray.

"Thanks' Stella." Renee carried the tray up the stairs. She met Emery on her way down. "Did you have a good ride?" She asked.

"I did thanks," Emery said with a slight smile. Her grey eyes narrowed as she studied Renee. "Is that for Cadi?" She asked, breaking the uneasy silence between them.

Renee nodded. "It is." Renee could feel her face flush, Emery's hard stare made her anxious. She breathed an inaudible sigh of relief as Emery stood aside and let her pass.

"Tell her I'll be up later with her medication."

Renee nodded, her heart raced as she hurried to Cadi's room. She could feel the nurse's eyes following her.

ဆဆဆ

Emery frowned as she watched Renee hurry away. She sensed a change in the young woman's attitude towards her. Her chest tightened as she descended the stairs and crossed the hall to the kitchen. Passing the dining room, she paused and peered in. No one was there. Wall paper had been stripped from one wall and white sheets covered the large dining table and most of the furniture. *I hope this doesn't take too long.* Walking over to a mirror she studied her image reflected in the glass. The thought of seeing him later gave her a strange warm feeling inside. Patting her short mousy hair in place, and running a tongue over her thin red lips, she grinned and strode into the kitchen.

Stella glanced up from her potato peeling. "Do you want some soup?"

"Yes thank you." Emery went to the pan and ladled a bowlful. "You carry on, I can do it myself."

Stella made no comment. Turning to the sink she continued with the potatoes. "Will you be in for dinner?"

Emery looked up from slurping her soup. "I will. I'm out this afternoon but only for a couple of hours. I shall go when I've given Cadi her medicine." Dropping her spoon into the empty bowl, she left the room letting the door slam behind her.

Staring at the door, Stella scowled. "Blast that woman."

Chapter 11

Dropping the legs of the tray, Renee placed it over Cadi's knees. Kneeling by the side of the bed, she gently stroked her sister's hand, it felt cold.

Opening her eyes Cadi smiled. "Hello,"

"Hello sweetie, how are you feeling?"

"Not too bad, my headache has eased." Pushing on her elbows she struggled to sit up.

"Wait Cadi, let me help you." Supporting her sister's weight, Renee fluffed the pillows and helped her rest against them. "Comfortable?" she asked.

Cadi nodded. "Yes, thank you."

"I've brought you some soup," Renee said, handing her the bowl.

"I'm not hungry but I will try."

"Good girl. I'll eat with you," Renee said taking her bowl. Her heart slumped as she watched Cadi struggle with the soup. It seemed lately she had more bad days than good. Lowering her eyes, Renee played with her soup. Seeing her sister like this took away her appetite.

Cadi's arms were matchstick thin, her eyes were dull…her face pale and ghost like. The hint of blue on her lips worried Renee.

Dropping her spoon in the bowl, Cadi looked at her sister. She could see the worry in her eyes but more than that, she saw fear. Sighing, she rested her head against the pillows. "How did it go with my Doctor? Is there any news about the scan?"

Renee shook her head. "No I'm afraid not. As far as he is concerned your condition is not serious enough to warrant a quick appointment."

"You are joking? How sick do I need to be?"

92

"As far as he's concerned at deaths door, I think." Dragging her hands through her hair Renee sighed.

Tilting her head Cadi studied her sister. "Is there more you're not telling me?"

"I'm afraid so. When I arrived at the surgery I saw your Doctor and Emery kissing. From what the receptionist told me they are married."

Speechless, Cadi stared at her…mouth wide open.

Renee patted her hand. "I'm sorry, but at least Emery doesn't know that I know."

Cadi shook her head, "You don't look too sure about that."

"I'll be honest I'm not. I met her on the stairs and she looked at me strangely, like she knew something I didn't." Slipping off the bed she paced the room. Stopping by the window seat, she gazed at the view allowing the beauty to calm her.

Hearing Cadi move she swung round.

Cadi raised her hand. "I feel awful getting you involved in all of this."

Renee hurried to the side of the bed. "I feel really bad telling you, because I know how much you like her."

"Yes I do, well I did, but now I'm not so sure. After what you've told me, how can I trust her?" Tears pooled in her eyes. "I can't."

Renee perched on the side of the bed. "I think we need to find you another Doctor as well. I really don't like that man." Lowering her head she played with her fingers. "He reminds me of someone, but I can't think who."

With a weary nod, Cadi slumped back against the pillows.

Renee took her hand. "I'm sorry about all of this." She wanted to ask if they should dismiss the nurse, but seeing her sister's distress decided against it.

Raising her head Cadi asked. "Are you any nearer to finding the key?"

"No luck yet I'm afraid. However, James was helping me search earlier, and he showed me some loose bricks in the fire surround. We both feel it's more than possible Ted hid the key somewhere in there." Seeing a spark of hope in Cadi's eyes, Renee smiled. "I can't wait to continue the search."

Cadi whispered. "Emery came in a few minutes before you arrived. She said she was going out, but I don't think she'll be long." Squeezing her sister's hand, she begged. "Please, Renee, go and take a look at the fire surround." Letting her head fall back on the pillows she raised a trembling hand and brushed tears from her cheeks.

Sniffing, Renee struggled to keep he own tears at bay. Seeing the state Cadi was in, angered and stressed her beyond words. Stroking her sister's hand, she said softly. "Don't upset yourself and above all stay calm. I'm going back to the library. Pray I have success and find the key." Rising to her feet she glanced at the tray. "You don't want this soup, do you?"

Cadi shook her head.

Picking up the tray Renee walked towards the door. Her brow wrinkled as she glanced back at her sister. She lay with her eyes closed. Her breathing sounded heavy...laboured. *Oh God, please help me. We must find that key and soon!* Hot tears wet her cheeks, her heart felt like a lump of lead in her chest. *I wish I knew what is going on here.* Closing the bedroom door she hurried down the stairs to the kitchen.

৶৶৶

Stella glanced at the open library door; she could hear Renee and James whispering…see them hurriedly pulling bricks from the fire surround. Flicking the duster over the highly polished hall table she prayed they would find the key.

She was never more relieved than when James offered to help Renee search. "Many hands make light work," she said rubbing vigorously at a finger print on the surface of the table. Every now and then she would pause and listen out for a car. The last thing any of them wanted was for Emery to return and catch them.

Stella sighed with relief. At last everyone believed her and felt the same about Emery. They were all on guard, eager to find out what was going on and why.

Moving to the library door, she whispered. "Any luck?"

James shook his head. "Not yet. But I have a feeling it's here somewhere."

"The question is where?" Renee said pursing her lips. Brushing a strand of damp hair off her face, she ran her sleeve across her forehead. "It is so flipping hot by this fire!"

"Stay calm pet. You'll find it I know you will." No sooner were the words out of Stella's mouth, than a sharp intake of breath from James made her jump.

Renee's heart leapt into her mouth as she peered at the small gap left by the brick in his hand. "What! What is it?"

"I can feel something," the excitement in his voice was contagious.

"Oh God please let it be the key," Renee whispered.

Stella pushed the door slightly. Her own heart thudded in her chest as she watched James carefully pull something out of the hole. She caught Renee's wide eyed gaze and returned her nervous smile. "Is it the key?"

"I think it is," Renee said.

In the silence that followed they watched James retrieve a package and slowly unwrap it. The atmosphere…the tension in the room was palpable.

Stella could hardly breath, wiping her sweaty hands on her apron she watched James hand a beautiful ornate key to Renee.

"I believe this could be what we've been looking for," he said his voice low and husky.

James came and stood beside Stella. They watched her take the key and go across to the door.

Stella held onto James's arm. She hardly dare look as Renee put the key in the old lock and turned it.

The resounding click as the lock responded to the key was never more welcome. All three of them sighed in unison as the door opened. With a loud sob Renee fell to her knees.

"Go to her James," Stella said pushing him forward. "I will keep an eye out for Emery." Closing the library door, Stella hurried to the kitchen. "I think we'll all need a cup of tea." *Or maybe something stronger* she thought as she put the kettle on to boil. Raising trembling hands heavenward she offered up a prayer of thanks.

Instinctively, she wanted to rush upstairs and tell Cadi, but that was Renee's privilege. Putting her hands over her heart, she slumped in a chair and allowed the excitement and tension to ebb away. *We must appear normal when Emery returns. Finding the key is our secret. Now, we will find out what that nurse is up to and we need to be quick for Cadi's sake.*

Fingering the loose fold of skin at her neck, Stella glanced at the kitchen door. She knew they weren't out of the woods yet, there were still so many questions and as yet no real answers. Stella's chest tightened uncomfortably as she struggled with the mystery of it all.

෨෨෨

Closing the small door, Renee locked it and pocketed the key. Sagging against the cool wood she stared long and hard at James. "I can't believe we've found it and only just in time." Resting her head against the door she allowed tears of relief to flow. "I don't know how to thank you."

James took her outstretched hands. "No need for thanks." Glancing at the library door, he whispered. "I have a feeling you may need me again. So know that I'm here for you."

Renee nodded and squeezed his hands, "Thank you." Moving away from the small door she glanced at the fire surround. "Did you put the brick back in place?"

James nodded. "I did." His eyes narrowed in a frown. "She'll have no idea we've found it."

Renee couldn't help smiling as she followed him to the library door. Her heart skipped a beat as she whispered, "I'm going upstairs to tell Cadi the good news."

"Okay, I'm going back to the stables. Be careful," he said staring into her upturned face. "And don't forget I'll help you in any way I can."

"Thank you," Renee said giving his muscular arm a grateful squeeze. Swinging round she took the stairs two at a time. Hurrying along the hallway she could hardly contain herself. *I must stay calm, everything needs to appear normal.* Pausing outside Cadi's room she took a deep breath, before gently knocking.

Propped against her pillows Cadi watched Renee approach. She could tell by her sister's expression…her confident gait, the sparkle in her eyes, something had changed. "You've found it, haven't you," she said indicating for Renee to sit beside her.

Perching on the side of the bed Renee fished in her pocket and handed Cadi the key. Leaning forward, she whispered, "We found it behind one of the bricks in the fire surround. Well, actually James found it."

Cadi clutched the key to her chest. Holding it tight in her fist she threw her arms round Renee's neck. "Thank you, thank you. You don't know what this means to me."

Pulling away, Renee stared into her eyes. "I think I do."

Cadi saw her expression darken. "What is it?"

Taking the key from her, Renee returned it to her pocket. "We have to act as though it's not been found." Gazing into her sister's eyes, she asked. "Can you do that?"

Returning Renee's gaze, Cadi nodded. "No problem. Did you go into the room?"

Renee shook her head. "No, you should be the one to go in there."

Cadi smiled and reached for her sister's hand. "Thank you Renee, for everything."

"You're welcome," Renee said gently brushing a strand of hair away from Cadi's face. Seeing her sister's frailty, she sighed. "We need to get in there soon but you won't be able to walk, you're too weak."

"I will," Cadi insisted. Finding the key and holding it in her hand had filled her with hope and a surge of strength she hadn't felt for some time.

Renee smiled and shook her head. "I don't think so. However, I have an idea. The next time Emery is out which I hope will be soon. I will get James to carry you down to the library." Renee paused and lowered her head.

"What?" Cadi asked.

"Once we've searched the room and God willing found something relevant to this situation. You need to get rid of Emery and I want to get you to the nearest hospital."

Cadi raised a hand in protest. "I can't get rid of Emery. If I do, how on earth will we trap her and her husband? We need to know what they are doing and why, and then we need to get the police involved. I'm well enough to cope for a bit longer," she said patting Renee's hand. "Whatever she is giving me is in a low dosage, merely enough to keep me incapacitated."

Renee nodded. "True, but that could change at any time. I need to get you away from here. You're going to have to trust me and James. If you can't find anything relevant in the room, he and I will have to keep searching until we do."

Cadi nodded. "Keep the key safe and well hidden."

"Don't you worry, I will." Rubbing Cadi's hand, Renee suggested they pray together. "We need God's protection over you and for Emery to leave the house, so that we have a chance to search that room. And it needs to be tomorrow."

Chapter 12

As much as they tried to keep a dampener on their glee over yesterday's success, still an atmosphere of suppressed excitement permeated the house. Renee prayed Emery wouldn't pick up on it.

Finding a safe place to hide the key had proved challenging. Renee had spent a restless night trying to sleep with the key under her pillow. Morning light streamed through the bedroom window, as she perched wearily on the side of the bed and stared round the room. There must be a good hiding place somewhere in here.

Glancing in the corner, she noticed a section of carpet was curled back. Wandering over she dropped to her knees and investigated. *This could be good.* Rising to her feet she retrieved the key and slipped it under the carpet. Then pulling a small easy chair away from the wardrobe she positioned it over the spot. Placing her hands on her hips she stood back and studied her handiwork. *It should be safe enough there, even if Emery sneaks in here I doubt she'll move furniture around.* With a satisfied smile, she took a quick shower before hurrying downstairs for breakfast.

"Good morning pet," Stella said with a cheery grin, as she set a plate of bacon and eggs in front of her. "How did you sleep?"

"Not too bad thanks." Sneaking a peek across the table Renee saw Emery glance at her. "How is Cadi this morning?" Renee asked. "I popped in to see her but she was asleep, so I didn't wake her."

Lowering her newspaper, Emery peered at Renee. "She seems a little better."

"That's good to hear, I'll pop up later."

"Do that." Folding the newspaper Emery rose to her feet. "I'm going for a ride. I'll look in on Cadi when I return."

Watching her leave Renee and Stella glanced at each other.

"How long do you think she'll be?" Renee asked.

Stella frowned. "She usually rides for a couple of hours but who knows. If you're taking Cadi into the library you'd best make it quick, just in case."

Renee nodded. "Have you seen Cadi this morning?"

"Ai pet, I took her up some breakfast."

"So how was she really?"

Noting the concern in Renee's eyes, Stella smiled. "When I got there, Emery was about to give her the medication. I could see Cadi was anything but keen. So I hurried over and put the tray in front of her. By the time I'd got the legs down and the warmer off the plate, Emery had backed off." Stella chuckled, "If looks could kill I would be dead."

"Did she say anything?"

"No, she just stood there clutching the glass and glaring. Anyway, I told her not to worry. I would make sure Cadi took the medicine once she'd had her breakfast. So she put the glass on the dressing table did a lot of huffing, and stormed out of the room. Naturally, I tipped the horrid stuff down the sink."

"Oh dear, that's a shame."

"Why?" Stella asked.

"Well, if you'd kept it we could have found out what Emery is giving her, because I'm sure it's not Cholestyramine. We could have had it tested, we need proof."

"I'm sorry pet, I didn't think. My first instinct was to throw the stuff away."

Seeing the concern in Stella's eyes, Renee smiled. "It's okay, don't worry. I'm sure we'll have a chance to get some more. At least my sister's had a reprieve this morning." Forking the last bit of bacon into her mouth, Renee pushed her plate away. "I'm going to wake Cadi, we need to take this opportunity and get her into that room."

Stella nodded. "If you want James he's in the dining room."

"Thanks, I'll retrieve the key first."

❧❧❧

Renee followed James as he carried Cadi downstairs and into the library.

James could feel Cadi tremble in his arms. "Are you sure you're okay miss?" he asked staring into her face. She felt light as a feather…a bony feather! Her face looked pale; a sheen of sweat beaded on her brow.

Staring up at him, Cadi smiled. "I'm alright, I'm just excited. I can't believe that at last I get to go into Ted's room." Turning her head she stared at the small door. Butterflies fluttered in her stomach. Reaching out she took Renee's hand. "I can hardly believe you found the key."

Renee squeezed her hand. "We don't have long, so I hope you can find something relevant pretty quickly."

Stella hovered at the library door her hands clasped to her chest. "Yes, be as quick as you can. I will listen for Emery's return but you need to hurry."

Renee shot her a reassuring smile. "Don't worry, just keep watch for us."

103

With a slight nod, Stella pulled the door to. Taking her feather duster off the table, she busied herself brushing it gently over the art work adorning the spacious hallway. The tension...having to keep her ears pricked for Emery's return, caused an unpleasant heart flutter. Praying quietly, she tried to keep herself busy and her mind occupied.

৯৹৹৹

Inside the library, the tension had upped dramatically. Cadi insisted on standing on her own two feet. "I'm okay James. I have waited so long for this day. I don't want to be carried into the room. I need to walk. Can you understand?" She glanced from Renee to James her eyes wide, questioning.

They both nodded.

"We don't want you to fall," Renee said holding out the key to her.

Cadi smiled and looked up at James. "If it makes you feel better just hold my arm." Reaching a hand to Renee, she took the proffered key.

No one said anything. The atmosphere was thick with anticipation. You could have cut it with a knife. Grouped close together, Renee and James watched, as with a trembling hand Cadi inserted the key into the lock and turned it.

The reassuring click made her heart skip a beat. Using two hands, she gripped the brass doorknob and turned it. As the door swung open the hinges creaked in protest. Raising a hand to her face she peered into the gloom.

Looking over her shoulder, James and Renee glanced at each other. The three of them realised it was not so much a room more a large cupboard. There were no windows. The only light afforded them came through the expansive library window. Dust, like a myriad little midges danced in the fractured light.

Cobwebs like torn lace curtains hung from the ceiling, their residents long gone.

The three of them paused on the threshold, their noses wrinkling at the musty smell of old books and documents.

"There must be a light in here somewhere," James said running his hand along the wall. His fingers touched a small hard case he hoped it was a light switch. Feeling a small button sticking out he flipped it down. Their unified sigh of relief echoed in the stillness.

"Oh my," Cadi said in a hushed tone.

"Where do we start?" Renee groaned.

Placing a hand on each of their shoulders, James said as confidently as he could. "It's not a big space. We'll break it into sections. Unfortunately, we can't split up as Cadi is the only one who possibly knows what she is looking for."

Cadi huffed and rolled her eyes at him. "I'm not much wiser than you two. I think we need to find official looking documents like a will, or solicitor's letters." Raising her hands, she stared around at the packed book shelfs, and old cupboards heaving with documents. "We must look for anything appertaining to this house and the estate." In the far corner she noticed an old desk with a swivel chair. "I need to sit down." Grabbing James hand she made her way to the seat.

Sighing with relief she sank into the chair and closed her eyes for a moment.

Renee knelt beside her, "Are you alright? Do you need to go back to your room?"

"No, Renee, let's see what we can find. We need to do a bit before Emery returns.

"Where should we start?" James asked.

Cadi's brow furrowed as she swivelled round on the chair. With three of them in the small space it felt claustrophobic. "There's so much stuff in here I don't know." Shrugging her shoulders, she suggested James start by the door and Renee could begin by looking through the cupboards.

Cadi turned the chair and faced the desk.

Hearing her sharp intake of breath, Renee asked. "What is it?" Cadi's wide eyed stare made her uneasy.

"Look," Cadi said pointing at a small white envelope. It sat on top of a pile of papers, blending in so well no one had noticed it.

Leaving the bookcase he was investigating, James leaned over Cadi's shoulder. "Goodness," he whispered. "It's addressed to you."

"It's Ted's handwriting," Cadi said as she gingerly picked it up. Her hand shook as she stared at it. For a moment the room seemed to spin. Raising one hand she clutched at the collar of her dressing gown. The other held the letter so firmly, it crumpled in her grip.

Easing her sister's fingers apart, Renee rescued the letter. "Do you want to read it now, or later?" She could see tears glistening in her sister's eyes. "Would you rather we wait in the other room?"

Cadi shook her head. Her voice quivered with emotion as she stared up at Renee. "I'll read it now," she said softly. Taking the letter from Renee she tore at the envelope. Pulling out two sheets of paper she glanced at James and Renee. "Stay with me," she said.

Pulling at his collar James stepped back, leaving the two sisters together.

Renee could see the flush of embarrassment on his cheeks. Giving him a reassuring smile she moved closer to Cadi.

Cadi's heart raced as she gazed at the hand written letter. Tears trickled down her cheeks as she laid the two sheets of paper on the desk and smoothed them out. Wiping her eyes, she sighed, picked up the first sheet and read. She felt as though Ted was there with her, in the room. The fine hairs on the back of her neck prickled. His written words spoke as if from the grave. The tenderness of his voice tore at her heart, while at the same time giving her cause to gasp with shock.

Renee averted her eyes rather than read over her sister's shoulder. She knew Cadi would share the relevant sections of the letter...the remainder was personal to her.

Facing James, she perched on the side of the desk. His troubled expression relayed the tension they all felt. Lowering her head she sighed and closed her eyes. The prospect of Emery's imminent return brought her out in a cold sweat. Glancing at Cadi she silently willed her to hurry. They needed to be out of the room as soon as possible.

Chapter 13

Cadi wiped beads of sweat off her forehead. Her whole body trembled with exhaustion. Clutching the letter, her heart raced as she tried to focus on her husband's words and ignore the anxious vibes from her sister perched on the desk beside her. As she read it was as though time stood still. Nothing and no one else existed. Ted's words embraced her, yet tore at her heart.

My darling Cadi,

If you are reading this letter, then you have found the key. Writing this was the hardest thing I've ever done, and I hardly know where to begin. However, first and foremost, I have no words to express the joy you brought into my life. Marrying you was the best decision I ever made. I love you and I always will. I'm so sorry our time together was shortened by the hand of evil. You may think I am being overly dramatic, but believe me I am not exaggerating.

There was a situation in my life that on reflection I should have shared with you, had I done so things might well be different. Forgive me for not fully trusting you. I was trying to protect you. Too late, I realised what a dreadful mistake I'd made. My need for secrecy has put you in danger. I pray to God if you are reading this, it is not too late. You have a right to know the truth. You need to know, for your own safety.

Raising her head Cadi breathed an inaudible sigh. Clutching her stomach she winced at a sudden griping pain. Feeling Renee's cool hand on her arm she glanced up.

"Are you alright?"

Cadi nodded as her eyes scanned the remainder of the letter.

"We need to hurry Cadi. Emery could return at any moment."

"I know I won't be a minute I've nearly finished." Hot tears pricked the back of her eyes as she glanced up at her sister.

Renee gave her a reassuring smile and gently squeezed her shoulder. Glancing across at James she shrugged at his questioning look.

Picking up the letter, Cadi instinctively clutched the collar of her dressing gown as she continued to read. A cold shiver went through her as she struggled to make sense of Ted's words. Seeing Emery's name in bold print increased the chill at her core.

Do not trust Emery my darling. I didn't know at the time, but she is the wife of my half-brother, Hugo. He's a Doctor at our surgery. He calls himself Mason, but his name is Grey. Cadi's hand shook so hard she stopped reading. Gasping, she lowered the letter. "I don't believe it, Doctor Mason is Ted's half-brother." Shaking her head she fixed Renee with a long hard stare.

Renee's hand flew to her mouth. "That explains why I thought he looked familiar. Read the rest Cadi as quickly as you can." Her heart raced as she watched her sister pick up the letter.

Cadi's eyes narrowed as she continued to read. *He is the result of my father's indiscretion with a woman he met in London while caring for my mother. She was ill, and in hospital. Believe me, I am not excusing what my father did…because of his actions our family payed an enormous price. When my mother eventually found out, the shock hastened her death. I was away at boarding school and had no real understanding of what was going on.*

After the loss of my mother, father changed. He became reclusive and suspicious of everyone. I was sent back to school and seldom allowed home. It's not a time I remember fondly. I missed my mother, and my close relationship with my father gradually deteriorated, until eventually we became strangers.

Sometimes, during the summer I would be allowed home. I remember on one occasion a strange woman arrived unannounced. She stood on the doorstep holding the hand of a small boy. My father refused them entry.

She came a few times, and on each occasion they would argue hotly. I would sit on the stairs out of sight. From what I overheard money was the cause of their disagreements. I found out later my father was paying for the boy's upkeep, but he refused to accept him as his legitimate child, meaning he had no rights of inheritance.

As you know, my father was the chairman of a large shipping company, and I imagine this woman was seeking to feather her own nest through her son. Before he died, father told me the woman had tried everything, including blackmail, to force him to accept his son. Personally, I believe he should have done. It wasn't the child's fault. He was used like a pawn between them.

However, after my father's death it was as though they disappeared off the face of the earth. To be honest, in the busyness of life I forgot about them. With you my darling by my side, life was good, until—"

"Quick! Someone's coming." James said edging away from the door.

"Who is it?" Renee hissed through clenched teeth.

James shrugged, "I don't know."

Cadi's heart raced as she roughly folded the letter, shoved it in the envelope and forced it into her dressing gown pocket. Her heart all but stopped as she glanced at Renee and James huddled behind the door.

Stella's sudden appearance brought a united sigh of relief. "Goodness, Stella you scared us," Cadi said.

"I'm sorry, but you need to get out of here. Emery has returned. I heard her trot round to the stables."

"Oh no, if she catches us in here, it's all over," Cadi said struggling to her feet.

"Don't fret," Stella said beckoning to James. "Quick, carry her to the couch by the fire."

Lifting Cadi in his arms, James carried her to the couch. Gently, he lay her down and wrapped a blanket round her legs.

Stella wiped nervous hands on her apron. "I'll make some tea and bring it in." Taking James by the arm she urged him to go back to decorating in the dining room. "If Emery sees you in here she will be suspicious." Pushing him out of the door she closed it and glanced anxiously at Renee. "What's wrong pet?" She asked, watching her struggle to lock the door.

Renee shook her head. "It's okay. The lock is stiff from lack of use but the key's turning now."

Clutching the blanket to her chin, Cadi whispered. "Please hurry, Renee."

Pocketing the key, Renee ran across the room and slumped on the couch beside her. "Phew, that was close." Renee gazed at Cadi, her brow wrinkled with concern. "Are you alright? You look pale."

"I feel a little nauseous, but I think it's all the excitement."

Renee reached a hand and gently touched her sister's forehead. "You're burning up." Twisting on her seat she looked up at Stella. "When you bring the tea, could you also bring a small bowl of cold water and a cloth?"

"Of course," Stella said hurrying to the door.

In the ensuing quiet, Renee watched Cadi relax against the cushions and close her eyes. She was desperate to ask about the letter but aware that Cadi needed to rest, she resolved to wait. Settling at the far end of the couch she fingered the key in her pocket. After all the tension, a strange but welcome peace pervaded the room.

Logs crackled and hissed in the flames of the fire. The ornate clock on the mantle shelf above, ticked softly, the hypnotic sound lulled her. Renee fought the desire to close her eyes. Stella's gentle tap on the door startled her.

"Sorry if I disturbed you pet," she said putting the tray on the side table. She smiled as Cadi opened an eye and peered at her. "How about a nice hot cup of tea, and I've brought some biscuits. I thought they might help with the nausea."

"Thanks Stella," Cadi said easing herself into a more upright position. "Where is Emery?"

Stella frowned, "She's gone to her room for a shower. So you can have some peace for a while longer." Taking a bowl of water and a cloth from the tray she handed them to Renee.

Renee doused the cloth, wrung it out and gently placed it on Cadi's forehead. "Hopefully, this will bring your temperature down."

Cadi nodded and smiled. Closing her eyes she embraced the comforting coolness.

Pouring the tea, Stella handed Renee a cup. "Did you find anything in there?" she asked nodding towards the small door.

"We did," Renee said softly. "Cadi found a letter Ted had left for her, but…"

"I didn't have a chance to finish reading it," Cadi said, as she handed Renee the now warm cloth. Lowering her voice, she said. "As soon as I have I will share it with you."

Renee glanced at Stella; both women could see the concern…the glimmer of fear in Cadi's eyes.

Pouring a cup of tea, Stella handed it to Cadi with a reassuring smile. "It's alright, pet. You mustn't fret. We will help you resolve this situation."

"And keep you safe!" Renee added.

Stella nodded, "Absolutely!"

As they continued to talk in hushed tones, Emery strode uninvited into the room. "Here you are," she said striding over to Cadi. "You weren't in your room, so I guessed I'd find you in here."

"You guessed right," Cadi said, unable to hide the sarcasm in her voice. "Why do you want me?"

"Well it will soon be time for your medication and I feel you should be upstairs resting."

Renee sucked in a noisy breath.

Scowling, Emery glanced at her before turning her attention to Cadi. "How did you get downstairs?" she asked.

"We got James to bring her down," Stella said. "You know she loves this room."

Cadi smiled at Stella. "I do, and I'm not ready to go up yet. So if you don't mind I would like to remain here with my sister."

Emery nodded, "Very well, but don't exhaust yourself."

Cadi pouted, "Don't worry I won't." *As if you would care if I did.* She smiled at the others as they watched Emery stomp from the room.

"I'm going to make some lunch," Stella said placing the empty cups and saucers on the tray. "Will you girls be alright?" Their enthusiastic nods brought a smile to her face as she left the room.

Moving close to Cadi Renee took her hand. "Are you sure you're alright?"

Cadi nodded. "I'm tired, but for the first time in months I feel positive. I know we will get to the bottom of this." Holding tight to her sister's hand, she whispered. "Soon, God willing, Ted will be avenged."

Wrapping her arms around Cadi, Renee held her close. "He will," she murmured in her sister's ear. "We will make sure of it."

ی‌‌یی‌ی

Emery banged a tight fist into her hand as she paced her room. She knew something was going on, but what? She had no idea and not knowing drove her crazy. *I don't care what he says; it's time to finish this.* With a growl of anger she went to the window and peered out. *I need to get into the library and find that key.* Throwing her head back she sighed with frustration. *It's there somewhere. I will find it and when I do!* The thought brought a smile to her lips.

Throwing her shoulders back she left her room and hurried down the stairs for lunch. She resolved, later that night she would leave no stone unturned in her effort to find the missing key. The thought of victory brought a flush of pink to her cheeks. Pausing for a moment at the bottom of the stairs she took a calming breath. Fixing a smile on her face she strode into the kitchen.

Chapter 14

Later that night, Renee stepped into the hallway and quietly closed her bedroom door. Pausing for a moment she took a few calming breaths and listened. All was quiet, and apart from a nightlight over the stairs, it was dark. Renee had paced her room for what seemed like hours, waiting for the sound of Emery's feet as she stole downstairs to the library. She had to pace, if not she would have fallen asleep, and missed the opportunity to get into Emery's room.

A slight frown flickered across her face, as she mulled over her conversation with Stella earlier that day, the house keepers reaction was not exactly positive.

"You're crazy," Stella had insisted. "Why on earth would you want to do such a thing?"

"I must. I need to try and find out what she is giving to Cadi. I'm convinced she is slowly poisoning her."

"I agree, but you're taking a huge risk. What if she returns and finds you in there. Oh pet, I don't think this is a good idea."

Watching Stella nervously twist her apron had done little for Renee's confidence.

"I'm sorry Stella, but I have to do it. I need to know." Wiping her hands on her trousers she sighed and lowered her voice. "But not only that, I must have some evidence."

Stella nodded, "I understand, but please promise you will be careful. This situation is disturbing enough as is it is. If she catches you in her room it could turn nasty."

"I know, but trust me I will be careful. I'm pretty sure she's going into the library tonight, she's getting desperate." Taking Stella's hand she said softly, "Pray for me."

"Of course I will. That goes without saying."

Standing in the dark hallway, Renee gained confidence knowing Stella would be praying for her. Apart from the strange noises all old houses make at night, it was quiet. Tilting her head she could hear vague sounds coming from downstairs. Her legs felt rooted to the spot, urging them to move she padded softly down the hallway. *Oh God, I hope she hasn't locked her door.* Dismissing the thought she hurried on.

Emery's door loomed large. A possible barrier to the truth Renee was seeking. She prayed it was unlocked. Her hand shook as she reached for the handle. To her relief it opened. Exhaling deeply she stepped inside and pulled the door to.

Reaching for the torch in her dressing gown pocket she switched it on. The soft light revealed a room strangely lacking in personal belongings. The bed was tidy and had not been slept in. An open suitcase sat on the ottoman at the end of the bed. Renee instinctively went to have a look being careful not to disturb anything, but there was nothing of interest. Looking around, from what she could see in the torch light, Emery appeared obsessively tidy.

Tip-toeing across to the bathroom she decided against switching on the light. Going straight to the bathroom cabinet she opened the glass door and shone the torch in. Every shelf was full of different items, medical and cleansing. Holding the torch with one hand she carefully investigated each shelf.

Rooting through the different items, she knocked a packet of facial wipes onto the floor. Flinching, her heart leapt into her mouth. Grabbing the packet she thanked God it was a soft item. Even though Emery wasn't in the room her whole body trembled with the tension. Her hand shook as she carefully put the packet back. *This is ridiculous! Trying to hold a torch and search one handed is hopeless.* Wiping her sweaty hand on her dressing gown, she continued searching, but found nothing. All the small cabinet contained were pain killers, plasters and numerous innocent medical stuff.

Chewing her lip, she groaned with frustration. Loath to give up she went to one of the dressing tables and started pulling out the drawers. Finding nothing she tried the smaller cabinet by the bed. Having searched the two top drawers she pulled open the bottom one. Carefully moving items of clothing around, her eyes settled on a brown bottle tucked at the back of the drawer. Holding it in the light of the torch she could see a few grains of powder in the bottom. There was no label on the bottle; nevertheless Renee knew it was what she was looking for. The small hairs on the back of her neck stood on end as she stared at it.

Straightening up, she placed a shaky hand over her mouth. Bile burned her throat. Hurrying to the bathroom she scooped cold water into her mouth. "Oh God, I think she is poisoning my sister, I'm sure she is."

Gazing at her reflection in the mirror she wiped a hand across her mouth. Staring at the bottle clutched in her hand, tears fell. Somehow, she had known it was true and yet seeing the evidence with her own eyes was too much to take in.

She stood rooted to the spot. She knew she should get out of the room but her legs refused to respond. Hearing a creak outside the door brought her to her senses. Hurrying into the bedroom she replaced the bottle where she'd found it. Every instinct screamed, take it to the police! But Renee knew if Emery found the bottle was missing she would do a runner, ruining any chance they might have of catching her and her accomplice husband. Not only that, Renee was sure it was poison, but with no label on the bottle how was she to prove it. No one would test it on her word alone?

Renee's heart felt like a lead weight in her chest as she tip-toed across the room, tilting her head she listened, but heard nothing untoward. Her hand felt sticky with sweat as she twisted the brass doorknob and peered into the darkness. Breathing a sigh of relief she stepped outside and closed the door.

Crossing the hallway to the darker side she melted into the shadows. Holding the torch close to her chest she could feel her heart pounding. There were two rooms to pass before she made it to her own. Staying close to the wall she moved as fast as she dare.

Seeing her bedroom door just ahead, she offered a silent prayer of thanks. But before she could move out of the shadows she heard heavy footfalls climbing the stairs towards her. An icy chill curled up her spine. Slinking back into a shadowed doorway she held her breath and waited.

She watched Emery shuffle wearily along the hall, her head down her shoulders hunched. It serves you right you murderous witch. Renee's grip on the torch tightened. An angry voice in her head urged her to rush the nurse, and use the torch to hit her over the head. Her lips pulled back in a silent snarl her hands shook with rage.

Nevertheless, she pushed the feeling down satisfying though the image was. Leaning further into the shadows she took a silent calming breath.

Vengeance belongs to God. He will repay. The thought comforted her as she watched Emery open her door and disappear inside. She hoped the woman would suss that somebody had been in her room…hoped the thought that the hidden bottle had been found would fill her with fear.

A slight smile touched the corners of Renee's mouth, as she padded softly along the hallway, and entered the safety of her room. Closing the door she leaned against it for a moment and breathed a sigh of relief.

৯৯৯

Emery sighed as she closed her bedroom door and leaned wearily against it. Switching on the light she straightened and stared round the room, a cold shiver ran up her spine. Something was wrong and she knew it. Clenching her fist she made for the small cabinet by her bed. Pulling the bottom drawer open she rooted through the contents. "Someone's been in here," she growled through clenched teeth. She could see the bottle of poison had been moved. Raising a trembling arm she wiped beads of perspiration off her forehead. Grabbing her phone she paced the room. "Come on, answer the damn phone!" Through her night wear she could smell her fear her nose wrinkled in distaste.

The sleepy voice on the other end did little to calm her. "Someone's been in my room," she hissed into the phone. "I'm sure they've found the poison, the bottle was moved. No it wasn't my fault! I was in the library looking for the blasted key." Her voice rose with frustrated anger. "Don't you shout at me, this whole thing was your idea."

Her brow creased in a frown as she listened to the person on the other end of the phone. Hearing him tell her this was the last of the poison and now was the time to finish the job, brought a sigh of relief from Emery. Her voice dropped to a whisper as she said, "Okay, you know the small woodland and the old folly up on the hill, bring the stuff and I'll meet you there tomorrow at five o'clock. I'll be riding, so conceal the car as best you can and stay undercover." Her lips pinched together as she listened and paced. The phone felt hot against her ear, as hot as the exasperated voice on the other end.

"Look, I've told you," she growled into the phone. "I will be riding. It's quicker and no one will think anything of it. I'm always out riding. Whereas, if I use the car it's going to arouse their suspicion, and if someone should see my car parked next to yours in the woods, it would definitely look strange." Pausing for a moment she hissed into the phone. "I'm riding! So make sure you're there on time."

Switching the phone off, she threw it on the bed and paced the room. Wrapping her arms round her middle, she tried to breathe normally. Knowing the poison she would pick up tomorrow was the last she would get was a great relief. Pressing her lips together she shrugged. *It's nearly over. I'm going to finish this. With Cadi out of the way, my husband can claim his rightful inheritance.* The thought of all that wealth brought a smile to her face.

❧❧❧

Standing at her bedroom window, Renee stared at the bleak yet beautiful landscape. Bathed in the light of an approaching storm it looked strangely eerie. Low clouds tinged with yellow scudded across the sky. The first drops of rain were accompanied by a streak of lightening. Knowing a thunder clap would follow, Renee drew back. She hated storms. If she was honest she feared them. At this precise moment the coming storm reflected her mood.

With a long sigh she lounged across her bed and slowly re-read Ted's letter. Her disturbed night had left her drained. "And now this," she said through clenched teeth. Clutching the letter she stared at the neat writing. "My God Ted, why didn't you say something?"

When Cadi had given her the letter, Renee had no idea what it contained. She'd seen the effect it had on Cadi, but she put that down to grief and reading her husband's words of endearment. Staring at the letter she could hardly believe what she'd read. Taking a deep breath she rolled onto her back and stared at the ceiling. Ted has a brother, I can hardly believe it! Huffing, she re-read the letter. The last few paragraphs were particularly chilling.

Ted had not seen his half-brother for many years. At the time he had no idea Emery was his brother's wife. As far as he was concerned she was a nurse sent by a local agency, and over time he grew to like and trust her. However, one day as he rested on the couch in the library he overheard Emery on the phone, and quickly realised the truth…something underhand was going on.

Renee's eyes blurred with tears. Wiping them with the back of her hand she continued reading. As she read, Ted's handwriting became more of a scrawl and harder to understand.

Realising I was in danger, he wrote, *threw me, my heart raced and the pain in my chest overwhelmed me. The strange weakness in my left side left me in no doubt…I was having a stroke.*

Overcome by what she was reading, Renee lowered the letter and tried to gather her emotions. "Poor Cadi, no wonder she is so distressed." Raising the letter she continued reading.

I reached for the bell to summon Stella, but then remembered she was out shopping with you, Cadi. I was on my own, but I knew what I had to do. I managed to reach the room behind the small door. My left arm and leg were useless, but I could still use my right hand, hence I am able to write this. Emery is out riding, nevertheless I must hurry.

Cadi, my darling, Emery is slowly poisoning me. I don't know what it is but I know I have little time left. My brother Hugo is behind this and when I am gone he will turn his attention to you. Oh my darling, I pray God you are safe and reading this. Keep Stella close and if at all possible ask Renee to come here and stay with you.

Please do not underestimate the danger you are in. Hugo and Emery are evil, clever and devious. It is too late for me, but you must save yourself.

I'm so sorry my darling; I should be there to protect you. May God keep you safe.

You are always in my heart.
Your loving husband,
Ted.

Dropping the letter, Renee buried her face in the pillow. The thought of Ted alone in the house, and dying; brought tears to her eyes. Muffled sobs racked her body. *Poor Cadi, how awful it must have been to come home and find him like that…such a shock.* Sitting up she grabbed a tissue and blew her nose. Going to the bathroom she splashed cold water on her face and stared into the mirror, puffy eyes stared back at her. Taking the hand towel she dried her face. "I need to pull myself together and stay strong," she muttered. "I know Emery is planning something, but what and when?"

❧❧❧

Emery knew she must act as normal as possible. Showering, she dressed quickly and made her way towards the stairs. Passing Cadi's room on the way to the kitchen she could hear voices, opening the door she walked in.

Renee was perched on the side of the bed helping her sister with her breakfast. "Good morning," she said cheerily, "And how is the patient this morning?"

"I'm alright," Cadi said without looking at her.

"Good to hear. After breakfast I'm going for a ride, I'll see you later." Striding from the room she closed the door and paused. She found their attempts to ignore her amusing. "Soon, they won't be so cocky." Puffing out her chest, she strode downstairs to the kitchen. "Tomorrow it will all be over." Glancing at the artwork adorning the walls her lips twisted in a grin. "Before long, all of this will be ours." Her eyes narrowed. "And I've earned it!"

❧❧❧

Renee placed Cadi's cereal bowl on the tray. "Have you had enough?"

"Yes, thank you." Cadi's brow furrowed as she stared at her bedroom door and said softly. "I wonder where she's going."

"I don't know, probably just for a ride. She seems to go most mornings."

"You're probably right but I'm glad she's going out."

123

Renee smiled, "Me too. While she's out do you want to go to the small room in the library? Stella will keep an eye out for us."

Cadi nodded, "That would be good. There is so much to sort out in there. Ted has so much paperwork."

Renee chuckled, "To say nothing of empty envelopes."

Cadi laughed, "I know."

Renee took her hand, "It's good to hear you laugh."

Squeezing her hand, Cadi said softly. "It's good to have you here. You give me the courage I need to face all of this. I know Stella's pleased you're here as well."

"I'm here for as long as you need me," Renee said rising to her feet. "I'll get James to come and fetch you."

"No need Renee, I think I can make it by myself."

"Are you sure? You have looked a little better these past couple of days, but you are weak."

"I know, but since I've managed to avoid taking some of that awful medication, I have felt better." Cadi stared at her sister. "What is it? You look worried."

Renee frowned, "I don't know, I just have a nasty feeling Emery is planning something."

Cadi nodded, "I agree but all we can do is try to remain vigilant. Stella will watch her in the kitchen, while we try to stay one step ahead of her up here."

Renee wiped her hands on her jeans. *Easier said than done*, she thought. Picking up the breakfast tray she headed for the door. Glancing back, she asked. "Do you want me to help you in the shower?"

"No thank you, I'll be fine."

"Okay, ring the bell when you're ready to come downstairs and I'll come and help you."

Cadi smiled. "I will thanks."

Chapter 15

Emery stood in the stable yard and gazed around. The early morning air was crisp and invigorating. A light frost on the rooves of the buildings sparkled in the early rays of the sun. Shivering, she yawned and wrapped her arms around her middle. Hurrying to the tack room she heard Bob and his son getting ready for work. Leaning over the tack room door she shouted for Bob.

Leaving the wheelbarrow he walked over to her. "Morning," he said.

Emery merely nodded. "I'm taking Major out." Straightening up she secured her riding hat.

Tilting his head to the side, Bob studied her. "You ride him most mornings."

"I know, but I wanted to tell you I will be riding again this evening, so don't rush to go home." She could see Bob's shoulders tense. Narrowing her eyes she attempted to hide her annoyance. "It won't be a long ride so you don't need to worry, but I want him tacked and ready for four thirty." She could see the curiosity in his eyes but ignored him.

"Do you want me to saddle him for you now?"

Emery shook her head. "No, I'll do it myself."

Shrugging his shoulders Bob turned away.

Smirking, Emery watched him retrieve the dung filled wheelbarrow. "You and your son will be the first I get rid of," she growled under her breath. Lifting Major's saddle down, she grabbed his bridle and hurried to the stable. Opening the door the warm smell of horse and hay greeted her.

Major snorted and pawed at the ground. His dark bay coat gleamed in the muted light of the stable. Emery smiled as she watched him shake his muscled neck. "Steady now," she said, her voice uncharacteristically soft. She liked Major and enjoyed riding him.

He stood quietly as she put his saddle and bridle on. "You enjoy our morning rides as much as me, don't you." Leading him out of the stable she gathered the reins and swung into the saddle. Urging him forward she walked out of the yard.

Seeing Bob unloading the contents of his barrow onto the muck heap, she guided Major over to him. "Don't forget I want him tacked and ready later today."

She found Bob's upturned face and quizzical expression amusing. She knew he was curious, as she seldom rode in the evening. Anxious to keep her activity a secret, she straightened in the saddle hoping to portray a composed and relaxed demeanour. "Do you have a problem with my request?"

Shaking his head, Bob turned away and continued shovelling the remaining manure onto the steaming muck heap. Glancing up at her, he said. "You know we leave at six. My wife doesn't like it when I'm late home."

Glaring at him, Emery snapped. "I told you, I'll be back long before you go." Snatching the reins, she turned Major and trotted away. Out in the open field she urged the horse into a canter. Glancing back she frowned, she could see Bob with his hands on his hips staring after her. "Get on with your work you suspicious old whatsit!"

Guiding Major towards the distant woods, her heart drummed with the beat of his hooves. The cold air rushing past took her breath away. She felt confident she'd chosen a good place to meet. So why were her insides quivering uncomfortably. *It will do no harm to check it out;* she thought as she slowed Major to a walk and guided him onto the forest path. Relieved to be out of the sight of prying eyes, she took a deep breath.

Glancing through the trees she could see the house in the distance. Captured in the morning light, the grey stonework of the old house appeared gold. Tossing her head back Emery grinned with satisfaction.

Reaching the place where she and her husband would meet later brought a contented sigh. "I knew this would be perfect. No one will see us here." Dismounting, she tied Major's reins to a branch and casually strolled around the clearing.

Stopping at one part of the clearing she rubbed her hands together. The natural pull in brought a smile to her face. "This is definitely big enough for one car. Any vehicle would be well hidden." Swinging round she clambered up a narrow rocky path. Once she reached the top she halted and took a few deep breaths. Placing her hands on her hips she stared at the familiar sight. The old ruined folly. Surrounded by trees the building looked strangely magical in the soft morning light. From the moment she'd first seen it, she determined that when she owned Five Acres the old building would be renovated. Glancing round she sighed with satisfaction. "I don't think anyone even knows it's here, accept me and my husband."

Chuckling to herself she returned to Major, untying him she swung into the saddle. Adjusting her reins she took one last look around. "He'll realize why I wanted to ride when he gets here. Another car would stick out like a sore thumb."

Satisfied that all would be well, she guided Major along a narrow path and they emerged out of the woods into open parkland. Shivering with the anticipation of success, she dug her heels into Majors flanks and cantered back towards the house, their pace quickly accelerated into a full gallop.

Giving an uncharacteristic whoop of delight, Emery urged the horse to go faster. The sound of his hooves drumming the ground, and the rush of cold air stinging her face made her heart race. She'd not felt this alive in ages. Nearing the stable yard she slowed him to a walk, straightening in the saddle she took a few deep breaths. The last thing she wanted to do was attract unwelcome curiosity.

The thought that soon she would be free to be herself brought a smile to her face. The only thing that dampened her pleasure was not finding the key to the small room in the library.

Shortening her reins she guided Major into the stable yard. For a moment her mouth tightened; failure to find the key was more than frustrating. She was sure Ted would have left some incriminating evidence, and she needed to find it. *Still, we'll soon get that door open when the house is ours.*

Reaching Major's stable she dismounted and tied his reins to the ring on the wall. "I'm back," she shouted.

James appeared from the tack room, "Okay, I'll deal with him." His eyes narrowed as he stared at the horse. "Looks like you've had a hard ride," he said, noting the white flecks of sweat on the horse's neck and shoulders.

Emery shrugged and turned away. "Have him ready for later this afternoon." Removing her riding hat she squared her shoulders and marched into the house.

❧ ❧ ❧

Leading Major into his stable, James made no reply. Grumbling to himself he removed the horses saddle and bridle, and with a handful of scrunched up straw began rubbing him down.

Bob leaned on the half door watching him. He could see the anger on his son's face. "She's run him hard."

James nodded, "He's too old and not fit enough to be run like that." He patted Major's neck, it felt cold and clammy. Covering the horses back with straw, he threw a heavy horse blanket on top. "That should warm him up." Joining his father they closed the top half of the door and walked to the tack room.

Bob grunted under his breath.

"What is it?" James asked.

"I feel I should tell Miss Cadi about the way her nurse is abusing old Major."

James handed him a coffee. "No don't do that dad. Miss Cady has enough on her plate at the moment. Leave it to me." Sipping his coffee he paced the small tack room. "It is strange her wanting to ride later." Turning to his dad his brow furrowed. "What do you think she's up to?"

Bob shook his head. "I don't know, but up to no good I bet."

Getting to his feet, James put his mug in the grubby old sink. "I'm going to see if I can have a discreet word with Renee. They need to know that something is going on."

Finishing his coffee, Bob stood. "Be careful son. We don't want to cause any trouble."

"Too late for that," James muttered under his breath. Frowning, he left the tack room and hurried towards the house. Apart from the usual sounds coming from the kitchen, the house was quiet. Removing his cap he ran a hand through his light brown hair. *Where is everyone?* Striding towards the dining room he opened the door and surveyed his handy work.

He wasn't a great one for decorating, but it didn't look too bad and it had accomplished what they'd planned…keeping him in the house and distracting Emery while they searched for the key. James rubbed his hands together and smiled, finding the key was one victory at least.

Leaving the dining room he went across the hall and tapped on the kitchen door. Hearing Stella's voice he opened it. "Is Miss Renee around?" he asked.

"Good morning pet," seeing the anxiety on his face, Stella wiped her hands on her apron, twisting the material between her fingers, she asked. "Is something wrong?"

James stood in front of the closed door fingering his cap. "I'm not sure," he said. "I need to speak to Renee."

"She is upstairs with Cadi. I'll go and fetch her. Help yourself to a coffee while you wait."

෨෨෨

Stella's chest tightened uncomfortably as she climbed the stairs. James hadn't said much but his expression spoke volumes. Reaching Cadi's door she gently tapped, peering inside she saw no sign of Renee, and Cadi was sound asleep. Quietly, Stella closed the door and walked along the hallway to Renee's room.

Further down the hallway she could see the door to Emery's bedroom. Her heart raced. She was grateful for the thick pile of the carpet. It muffled the sound of her feet. Nevertheless, she slowed her pace and crept towards Renee's room. Tapping lightly on the door she waited.

Hearing Renee's muffled response; she opened the door and went in. Renee was sat on the window seat. Stella rubbed her hands together as she hurried towards her. As she drew close she could see the concern in Renee's dark eyes.

"What is it Stella? You look worried."

"James needs to speak with you urgently."

"Where is he?"

"He's waiting in the kitchen," Stella said gesturing towards the door.

"Bring him up here Stella." She could feel heat rise on her cheeks as she noted the housekeeper's raised eyebrows. "You are to come with him," she added quickly. "It's just that in here we will have more privacy." Perching on the edge of the window seat she glanced out of the window.

Smoothing her apron, Stella moved closer to Renee. "What if Emery sees us in the hallway?"

Renee turned and touched her hand. "Don't worry. If she does all you need to say is you're showing him a job that needs to be done."

"But that's not—"

Renee stood to her feet. "I know it's not true Stella, but we have to do something. My sister's life could be on the line."

Renee's abruptness caused Stella to step back. "I know, and I'm sorry pet. I'll go and fetch James." Going to the bedroom door, Stella carefully opened it and stepped into the hallway. Glancing up and down she hurried towards the stairs. Her heart raced, what with all the intrigue and then nearly insulting Renee she could hardly breathe. Clutching at her blouse she all but ran to the kitchen.

James glanced up as she rushed in. Leaving his chair he asked. "Are you alright Stella?"

"I'm fine. Come with me, you can speak with Renee upstairs in her room. We're hoping it will be more private." Beckoning with her hand she led him towards the stairs. Pausing at the bottom she glanced at him. "Should we bump into Emery follow my lead. I'm showing you a job that needs doing in one of the rooms, okay?"

James nodded as he followed her up the stairs.

৯৯৯

Chewing her bottom lip, Renee paced her room. *I wonder what James wants to tell me?* She couldn't imagine it would be good news. Hearing a soft tap on the door she hurried to open it. "Quick, come in." Closing the door she whispered, "We need to keep our voices down." Ushering them to the small settee and chair by the fire, she fixed James with a penetrating stare.

Twirling his cap between his fingers he returned her gaze. "I'm sorry to bother you Renee, it could be something or nothing, but I need to know what you think.

"Tell me," Renee said trying to hide the impatience in her voice.

James leaned forward in his chair his eyes fixed on both women. Lowering his voice, he told them what Emery had said to his father. "She seldom rides in the late afternoon, especially now the nights are drawing in, but she was insistent that Major be tacked and ready for four thirty." Rubbing a hand through his hair he leaned back in the chair. Looking at Renee, he shrugged his shoulders. "So, what do you think, should we be worried?"

Renee glanced at Stella, the housekeeper was doing what she always did when anxious...clutching at her apron. Renee gently nudged her. "What do you think?" She asked.

Sighing, Stella said softly. "I'm thinking the same as you," she glanced across at James, "both of you." Looking towards the door her brow furrowed. "Whatever she has planned, it's going to take place tonight, or tomorrow, and we need to be ready."

James nodded and leaned closer. "Right, well we need a plan and it's going to have to be a good one."

"Do you have something in mind?" Stella asked.

"Actually, I do, but it will take some arranging and we'll all have to be involved, including dad."

The gleam in his eye's filled Renee with confidence. Resting her head on the back of the settee, she waited to hear his plan.

♥♥♥

Leaning forward in his chair, James rested his arms on his thighs. Twirling his cap between his fingers, he lowered his head and stared at the floor.

"So what are you thinking?" Renee asked.

"Give me a minute. I need to collect my thoughts." He could feel Renee's impatience, but he needed to get the plan clear in his head before sharing it. Straightening in his chair he took a deep breath. "We need to follow Emery, or at least one of us does."

Renee sighed. "How can we do that she will see us?"

"That's why it will have to be me," James said.

"I don't understand, why you?" Renee asked.

James shrugged. "Because I think I know where she is going."

"You do?"

James smiled at Renee and nodded. "Yes, there's an old folly in the woods. I've been there a few times clearing shrubbery and collecting fire wood for the house. Emery has turned up on numerous occasions but I've kept out of sight. She thinks the folly is her secret place."

Seeing Stella's surprised expression, James relaxed back in his chair and chuckled. "I don't even think Miss Cadi knows about the folly."

Stella pursed her lips and shook her head. "I had no idea there was a folly on this land. Cadi has never mentioned it."

"She obviously doesn't know, but I bet she'll be thrilled when she finds out," Renee said.

Raising his hands, James called them to order. "Let me tell you the rest of my plan because you all have a part to play." Seeing Renee's narrowed eyes, James smiled. "Sorry, I don't mean to be bossy, but we don't have much time."

"True," Renee said. "We're all ears so carry on."

Seeing he had their attention, James continued. "I'll saddle Berti and ride out to the woods. If I leave at three thirty, I can hide in the trees and intercept her when she leaves after doing whatever it is she's doing."

"What about us?" Renee said glancing at Stella.

Facing Stella, James told her to watch for when Emery leaves the house. "When she's gone, put Miss Cadi in the car and drive her to the hospital." Seeing Stella's wrinkled brow, James asked. "Is there a problem? Your car is parked in the lean-to."

"It's been standing there ages," Stella said. "What if it doesn't work? What if the battery is flat?"

Renee touched her arm. "It's not a problem you can use mine."

Stella patted her hand. "Thanks Pet. Yours would be more reliable."

Turning to James, Renee asked. "So what about me, what should I do?"

Leaning back in his chair, James said. "Dad doesn't know it yet but he's going to help us." Noting Renee's raised brows he smiled. "Don't worry. He'll be fine about it." He leaned forward. "Renee, I need you and my dad to drive to the main entrance and block it with his Land Rover. Whoever is meeting Emery will be driving and there's no other way out of the estate. So they are going to have to leave by the main entrance." Pausing, he fingered his cap. "This is important. Before you leave the house ring the police. Tell them drug users are on your land which should get them here pretty quickly."

"That's no problem, but what time should Bob and I leave the house?" Renee asked.

"You need to get there after this person has already driven into the woods. The last thing you want to do is meet them on the road."

"Exactly, that would be my concern." Renee said.

"Don't worry, Emery wants Major ready for four thirty. I'm pretty sure she's going to the folly which is about twenty minutes from here. So if you and dad get to the main gate by five fifteen that should be fine. I think that's everything," he said rising to his feet. Raising a finger he added. "There is one thing. I don't know if you will both agree, but I think it best not to tell Miss Cadi about this."

Looking from one to the other he was pleased to see their nods of agreement.

Touching his arm, Renee said softly. "Thanks James, it's a good plan and I think it will work."

James smiled. "I'm glad you agree. God willing this will soon be over and Miss Cadi will be safe."

With a nod of agreement, Renee opened her bedroom door and checked the coast was clear. She watched as Stella led James along the hall and down the stairs.

James followed Stella to the back door. Before leaving he took her gently by the shoulders. Staring into her upturned face he could see the concern in her eyes. "It'll be alright Stella don't worry. You get Cadi to the hospital and leave the rest to us. As soon as Emery leaves take Cadi to the car, Renee will have time to help should you need it."

Lowering her head Stella twisted the front of her apron.

"What is it?" James asked. Rubbing the back of his neck he glanced around…worried. Emery might appear at any moment.

Stella clutched his arm. "I'm sorry James, but I'm afraid Emery will see my anxiety."

James took her hand and squeezed it. "Don't think about it just try to act normally."

Stella pulled the bolt across and let James out. "I'll try, see you later."

James nodded and hurried across the yard to the stables. Bob was waiting for him in the tack room.

"So how did it go?"

"It went okay, between us we've come up with a plan which I think will work." For the next half hour James shared it with his dad.

Bob sat in a chair listening intently. His heart raced with anticipation.

Sitting across from him, James rested his arms on his thighs. Seeing the excitement in his dad's eyes, he knew he was pleased to be taking part. He was an old man, but even to this day James knew he could handle himself. "You may not need it, but just in case take the shotgun." Leaning closer he whispered. "Please be careful, whoever Emery is meeting could also be armed and you'll have Renee with you. I don't want either of you to get hurt."

"Don't you worry son, no one is going to get hurt. You can rely on me. They won't get out of this estate either, not alive anyway."

James's brow shot up, "Dad!" he exclaimed.

"Oh don't worry son, I'm only kidding."

"Glad to hear it," James said. Running a hand through his hair he stood up. "Come on we need to get some work done, everything has to look normal."

Chapter 16

Renee paced her room, excitement mixed with apprehension made her stomach churn uncomfortably. It was all happening so fast. Rubbing the back of her neck she stared out of the window. A watery sunshine filtered through the clouds. It wasn't a bad day…the sort of day she liked to walk. However, she knew she must stay around the house. She dare not let Emery out of her sight. "It's going to be a long day," she muttered as she grabbed a cardigan from the wardrobe.

Opening her bedroom door she stepped into the hall, closing it quietly she listened for a moment. She could hear Emery moving around in her room. Renee smiled, *she's probably packing*. Padding along the hall Renee stopped outside Cadi's door and tapped. Cadi's muted voice called her in.

"How are you?" Renee asked.

Sitting on the side of the bed, Cadi raised her head and smiled. "I don't feel too bad. Raising her hands she stared at them. "But I hate the way these look and I still feel a little nauseous."

Renee sat beside her, "Don't worry you'll soon be well."

"I hope you're right."

"I am," Renee said putting an arm round her. "Do you fancy a coffee in the library?"

Cadi grinned. "That would nice. Give me a minute to get dressed." From the bathroom she shouted, "Have you seen Emery this morning?"

"Only briefly, she's in her room." Renee lounged back on Cadi's bed, her mind whirring as she thought about the events later that day. Keeping it from Cadi would not be easy.

Coming out of the bathroom Cadi stretched out her hand. "Come on then let's go I need a coffee."

Grabbing her sister's outstretched hand Renee followed her to the stair lift and helped her onto the seat. Slowly it trundled down to the hallway. Renee supported her as they walked to the library. Helping her onto the couch she tucked a blanket round her legs. "Are you warm enough?"

Cadi nodded.

"Okay, I'll go and find Stella and bring us some coffee." As Renee approached the kitchen Stella's head appeared round the door. "I thought I heard voices. I suppose you want some coffee," she said with a twinkle in her eye.

"Yes please," Renee said following her into the kitchen.

"How is Cadi?"

"She's seems a little better, but the sooner we can get her to hospital the happier I will be."

"Me too pet; I can't wait for Emery to leave the house so that I can take her." Stella sighed as she poured boiling water into the coffee pot. "I'm finding it hard to act natural around Emery."

"Don't worry Stella it won't be long now. Just try and keep out of her way." Stella nodded, but Renee could see the doubt in her eyes. Patting her hand she took the tray of coffee. "I'll see you later, stop worrying."

Pursing her lips, Stella opened the kitchen door for her. "I'll see you at lunch time," she said softly.

Renee nodded.

و~و~و

The day seemed to drag and the loud tick of the grandfather clock in the hall amplified Renee's sense of doom. Looking at her watch for the hundredth time, she sighed. It was three thirty.

Her heart raced as she thought of James riding Berti to the woods. He was going to have a long wait. "I hope Emery doesn't see him," she muttered as she put on a warm jumper. Hurrying downstairs to the kitchen, she found Stella busy wiping down the work surfaces. Renee smiled at the relieved expression on her face. "It's nearly time to take Cadi to the hospital," she said glancing at the kitchen clock. "James must be in the woods now."

Stella nodded. "Where is Cadi?"

"She's resting in her room. You mustn't worry. As soon as Emery leaves I'll help you get her into the car."

"Oh thanks Pet. I don't think I could manage her on my own."

"I know, but once you reach the hospital there will be people there to help you." Renee sighed. "It'll be such a relief when she's away from this house and safe."

"It certainly will," Stella said. "And don't forget to ring the police."

"Don't worry I won't forget."

ૐૐૐ

Bob sat in the tack room, his thoughts centred on his son. He'd watched James saddle Berti and ride off towards the woods. "I hope that witch doesn't see him," he muttered. Loading the shotgun he laid it across his lap and busied himself wiping it down with a rag.

141

Glancing at the wall clock he frowned; it was four fifteen. Leaning the shot gun against the wall he listened for Emery's arrival. Major was saddled and tied outside the stable. *All she's got to do is mount up and go.* As the thought entered his head he heard footsteps.

Leaving the tack room he stood in the doorway. "As requested, he's ready."

Emery nodded but made no reply. Untying the horse she swung into the saddle and trotted out of the yard.

Bob scowled at her retreating form. "You wait lady," he muttered under his breath. Grabbing the gun he hurried to his old land rover and put the gun on the back seat. It would soon be time to leave. He prayed Renee would be on time.

Driving to the front of the house, he parked behind Renee's car and waited. Seeing the front door open he breathed a sigh of relief. He made to leave his car and help Renee and Stella with Cadi, but Renee held up a hand and mouthed, "We're okay."

The two women guided Cadi to the car. She was weak and leaned her whole weight on them, but between them they settled her in the front seat.

Cadi looked up at Renee. "Why aren't you coming with us?" She grabbed Renee's hand. "I'm scared, what if Emery sees us."

"I'm sorry Cadi I can't come and Emery won't see you so don't worry." She glanced over at Bob. "Bob and I have something important we need to do. Stella will take care of you and I'll come to the hospital as soon as I can." Fixing her sister's seat belt she ignored her inquiring stare and gently kissed her on the forehead. She looked across at Stella. "Drive safely."

"Don't you worry, pet. I'll take care of her." Stella started the car and slowly negotiated the long gravel drive.

Rubbing her arms, Renee watched until the car was no more than a speck in the distance. Hearing Bob call her she wiped her eyes and joined him.

"I'm sorry miss, but we need to go. If he's coming he'll already be in the woods." Bob turned the key in the ignition and drove towards the main gate showering gravel in his wake.

"I'm sorry for holding you up Bob. I'm finding this whole situation so hard."

"I understand miss but don't you worry about your sister, she's safe with Stella, and once she's in hospital they'll sort her out. It's up to us now to catch the perpetrators." Reaching the gate, Bob swung the land rover across the entrance blocking anyone from getting in or out. Climbing out of the vehicle, he opened the rear door and retrieved the shot gun. "Did you ring the police?" he asked Renee.

She nodded, "They're on their way."

"Good, did they say how long?"

"The officer I spoke to said it would take about forty five minutes to get here."

Leaning against the vehicle, Bob glanced at Renee. "We can hold him for that long and if he tries anything." He patted the gun resting in the crook of his arm. Seeing the shock on Renee's face he smiled. "Don't you worry miss, I've never shot anyone and I don't intend to start now. However, he doesn't know that." His chuckle was contagious, Renee couldn't help laughing. It broke the tension and helped her to relax.

ॐॐॐ

Emery urged Major into a gallop; she couldn't afford to be late. Cold air rushing past stung her face and yet she felt hot...panting to get her breath. "I'll be glad when this is over," she muttered through clenched teeth.

Pulling back on the reins she slowed Major to a walk and guided him in among the trees. She could feel his flanks heaving against her legs. Sweat glistened on his neck. Grimacing, she pushed the guilt aside. Pulling him up she slid to the ground and tied him to a low branch. "You can rest awhile now," she said patting his shoulder. It felt cold and damp under her hand. Turning away, she saw her husband's car and grinned.

Her legs trembled slightly as she negotiated the steep climb up to the folly. Her husband turned as she approached and walked to meet her. Raising a hand she quickly said, "I'm not late."

"I didn't say you were." Putting his hand in his pocket he retrieved a small brown bottle. "This is the last of it. I suggest you do it tonight. She'll be sick and delirious but it shouldn't last long. You can put her death down to something she's eaten."

Emery stared into his cold dark eyes. She tried to swallow the lump in her throat.

Hugo smiled, "You're not going soft on me, are you?" Stroking his neatly trimmed beard he studied her. Then taking her hand he squeezed it. "It's nearly over, we are in the clear."

Emery winced at the pressure of his hand.

With a menacing edge to his voice, he said. "Don't let me down."

"I won't," Emery snapped. Pulling her hand free she glared at him. "The fact we've got this far is down to me."

His eyes softened as he pulled her into a hug. "I know," he said softly.

Emery's breathing quickened as she gazed into his face. She couldn't fight the hold he had over her. The hairs prickled on the back of her neck as he softly kissed her cheek. "Don't worry," he whispered in her ear. His warm breath sent shivers down her spine.

Releasing her he stepped away. "You'd better go back to the house before you're missed." Making a wide gesture with his arm, he gazed around. "After tonight, all this will be ours."

Emery smiled and with a nod hurried down the steep bank to Major. Fingering the bottle in her pocket she tried to ignore the unpleasant quiver in her stomach.

Looking up she watched Hugo negotiate the bank. He gave her a cheery wave as he got into the car. Emery stuck out her chin and ignored him. As he drove past he winked at her. Frowning with exasperation Emery untied Major and swung into the saddle. *It's alright for him. I'm the one who has to do the dirty work.* Shortening her reins she guided Major out of the woods.

Shaking her head, Emery closed her eyes for a moment. Patting the bottle in her pocket she smiled. But her relief was short lived. She stiffened in the saddle as James appeared out of the woods and blocked her path.

৯৯৯৯

James stood among the trees, not far from the path he knew Emery would use to leave the woods. Holding Berti on a loose rein he let the horse graze. He prayed when Major appeared Berti wouldn't give the game away.

It was getting cold, he was glad of his coat and cap. Tilting his head he listened, apart from the birds, and the soft rustle of leaves in the breeze, all was quiet. Earlier he'd heard a car so he guessed Emery's husband had arrived. Not long after he saw Emery galloping across the park and disappear into the woods.

Thinking of the way she treated Major his lip curled. *Being ridden so hard is not good for the old boy.* Curling his hand into a fist he tried not to think about it. Patting Berti he breathed a sigh of relief, soon God willing she would be gone.

As the sun began to set and the air grew colder, James shivered and pulled his coat close. Looking at his watch he frowned. "I hope they're not going to be much longer," he whispered to Berti. Seeing the horse's ears flick and hearing a car engine burst into life, he gathered the reins and swung into the saddle.

James knew he must stop Emery on the path. If she got ahead of him he would never catch her. Berti would never keep up with Major. As he urged Berti closer to the path he felt tightness in his chest, his breathing accelerated. He hadn't expected to be nervous and it annoyed him. "She's a woman," he growled. "What can she do?" The words renewed his confidence. Sitting straight in the saddle he took a deep breath and waited.

Chapter 17

Hearing the sound of a car engine, Renee moved closer to Bob. Giving her an encouraging smile he cocked the gun. Renee's eyes narrowed as she stared at it. She hated guns and loud bangs. Nevertheless, she knew the gun gave them the advantage they needed. Following Bob's gaze she stared towards the woods. Wiping her sweaty hands on her jeans she waited for the car to appear.

Bob took her by the arm and guided her to other side of the vehicle. Seeing her quizzical expression, he said. "He won't see us, or the car parked here until it's too late. I don't want him driving all over the estate in a bid to escape. We need to hold him here until the police arrive."

Renee nodded. "Good thinking, but how will you stop him if he does try to escape?"

Bob glanced at her and grinned. "Oh I have a plan, but don't worry, it doesn't involve shooting him, much as I would like to." Before Renee could say anything Bob pulled her down beside the car.

"What?" Renee hissed.

"He's driving towards us. You'd best stay here miss."

Renee frowned as she watched him walk round the Land Rover. She hated being told what to do. *This is my sister we're trying to help and no one is going to stop me getting involved.* The thought galvanised her. Standing up she watched Bob raise the gun. Her heart pounded, she wanted to call to him but remained silent.

Pointing the shotgun at the approaching car, Bob waited for it to stop. It was moving fast but he held his ground. As the vehicle came closer Bob could see the drivers face…white with anger.

Putting a hand to her mouth, Renee ran and stood beside Bob.

The car skidded to a stop, gravel and grass spraying in its wake. Glaring, and shouting expletives the driver scrambled out of the car.

"What the hell do you think you're doing? Move that vehicle I need to get out of here."

"I'm sure you do," Bob said. "However, we are waiting here for the police."

"What do you mean, Police! What are you talking about?"

Renee stepped towards him, but Bob grabbed her arm and held her back. "We know who you are," she shouted. "Your name is not Mason, it's Grey, and you're a murderer."

"What are you talking about you stupid woman. I haven't murdered anyone."

"No, but you made it possible for Emery to do it. With her help you killed my sister's husband… your half-brother Ted Grey. And now you're trying to kill her."

"I'm not trying to kill anyone and what half-brother? I don't have a half-brother."

"You're a liar. He's dead because of you. You murdered him. She watched him pull at his collar. She knew she'd struck a chord. He was guilty as hell. Beads of sweat glistened on his top lip.

Hugo glared at her. Wiping his lip with the back of a hand he took a step towards her.

Bob stepped in front of Renee the gun pointing at Hugo's chest. "Stay where you are. As we speak your wife Emery is being intercepted and when the police get here the truth will come out."

Raising his arms, Hugo shouted. "The truth is you are both mad! I haven't murdered anyone."

"We'll see about that when the police arrive," Renee said moving to stand beside Bob.

Balling his hands into fists Hugo growled with frustration. Eyeing them both he wondered what his chances were if he rushed them. After all it's just an old man and a young woman. *I could take them both…easy.* But seeing the way the old man held the gun and the confident glint in his eyes, Hugo dismissed the thought. Relaxing his shoulders his lips twitched in a smile. *They can't prove a thing.*

Jutting her chin, Renee glared at him, furious at his relaxed posture and supercilious grin. Thinking of Cadi and all she'd been through, Renee longed to knock the stupid smile off his face.

But the desire to strike him vanished at the sound of thudding hooves and angry shouts. The three of them turned to see Major galloping towards them. Emery was using her riding crop to keep the horse going. Shouting and waving his arm, James pushed Berti to keep up with Major.

ই৯ই৯ই৯

As soon as Emery appeared, James urged Berti onto the path blocking her way. James couldn't help smiling at the surprised look on her face. The colour had drained from her cheeks, her eyes widened as she stared at him.

"What are you doing here?" She shouted. "Get out of my way."

"You're not going anywhere," James said, his voice low and menacing. "We've found out what you've been doing. You and your husband are murderers. You killed Miss Cadi's husband and now you're attempting to kill her."

Emery's eyes narrowed as she glared at him. "What are you talking about?" Her voice rose as she shouted, "I haven't killed anyone." The blush rising on her neck and face, the whiteness of her knuckles as she gripped the reins were enough to convince James…she was lying.

"We know you met your husband up at the folly. He's given you something and I want it."

"What could I possibly have that you would want? Get out of my way farm boy." Nevertheless, Emery's hand shook as she nervously touched the pocket containing the small bottle of poison.

James smiled as he moved Berti closer and held out his hand. "You and your husband are not leaving this estate. The police are on their way, so you may as well give me what's in your pocket. If you don't I will take it from you."

"I'll give it to you alright," Emery said raising the crop.

Before James could move his outstretched hand, Emery brought the riding crop down with a stinging blow. With a cry of pain, James pulled his hand away and held it to his chest. One handed he tried to control Berti.

Both horses startled by his loud cry, panicked. Major surged forward forcing Berti off the Path. Shaking his head from side to side Major fought against Emery's tight hold on the reins. She continued to swing the crop catching Berti on the side of the neck. The horse reared and backed further into the trees, clearing a way for Emery to escape.

Major shot forward as the crop bit into his shoulder. Emery hung on as the panicked horse thundered along the path and out of the woods. Grass and mud flew in the air as he galloped for home.

Looking behind, Emery saw James emerge from the trees."

Using his reins, James urged Berti to keep up with Major, but the big hunter pulled away lengthening the distance between them.

Emery grinned, "You're wasting your time farm boy." Something made her glance towards the main gate of the property. Seeing her husband's car and a group of people her heart dropped, beads of sweat glistened on her forehead. Tightening the reins she tried to pull Major round. Shaking his head he fought her. Cursing, she hit him on the neck and yanked hard on the reins. Without slowing he swung round and galloped towards the gate. Using her crop on his quarters she urged him on.

Her lips tightened as she neared the gate. Her husband stood by his car with his hands in the air, his eyes glued to the shot gun held by Bob. Behind her she could hear James yelling, it spurred her on. She had no idea what she was going to do only that she must help her husband. If they couldn't succeed in their plan then they must get away.

Turning Major, she galloped him towards Bob, screaming at her husband to get out of the way. If the situation had not been so dire, she would have laughed at their facial expressions. Bob's eyes bulged as he turned to face her. Renee squealed and tried to pull Bob out of harm's way. While her husband, his face as white as a sheet frantically waved his arms and shouted for her to stop.

ఇఇఇ

The short sharp burst of a siren and the sound of a car skidding to a halt added to the confusion.

Renee and Bob swung round to look. Relieved to see two burly policemen get out of the car and run towards them.

Seeing his wife nearly upon them and his captors distracted, Hugo rushed Bob and made a grab for the gun. Hanging onto it he wrestled the older man to the ground, punching him in the face. The gun discharged missing him by inches. His ears rang and for a moment he heard nothing. Red faced his eyes bulging. He yanked the gun out of Bob's hands and stepped back towards his car.

His hands were shaking, tightening his grip on the gun he stared around. His attention was caught by Renee; her eyes were wide and glued to the other side of his car. She stood with her arms wrapped around herself... rocking and whimpering; tears streamed down her face. A police officer held onto her while the other slowly approached him, stopping when Hugo turned the gun on him.

"Let me have the gun sir."

"Stay back," Hugo snarled. Frowning he put a hand to his ear, someone was screaming it was coming from the other side of his car. The sound was deafening...unearthly. It hurt his ears. Glancing down he saw Bob half-conscious on the ground with a young man kneeling beside him.

Out of the corner of his eye he saw the officer move, swinging round he pointed the gun at him. "I told you, keep away." Running a jerky hand through his hair he gulped a deep breath. *My wife was galloping towards us.* The remembrance brought him out in a cold sweat.

He glanced around. "Where's my wife?" His voice trembled as he pointed the gun at the officer's chest. "Where is she?"

The officer held out his hand. "There has been an accident sir, if you give me the gun I will explain."

Hugo stared at him. He found the soothing quality of his voice disturbing. He knew without being told something had happened to his wife. The tightness in his chest increased he could hardly breathe. Keeping the gun pointed at the officer he backed towards the rear of his car.

The police officer moved towards him. "No sir, don't go there."

James joined the officer. "Listen to him," he said.

Hugo held the gun in trembling hands as he glared at them. "Where's my wife he shouted?" James's fleeting look towards the other side of the car didn't go unnoticed by Hugo. With one eye on the two men, also Bob now on his feet and standing behind them, Hugo knew he had no chance. Sooner or later they would disarm him. However, for the moment he had the upper hand. Ignoring their demands that he drop the gun, he moved slowly around the back of the car and came to an abrupt halt.

He stared open mouthed at the scene before him. An icy coldness chilled him to the bone. Bitter bile rose in his throat. Unable to move or make a sound he stood there. The gun slipped unnoticed from his hand and lay in the grass. The eerie silence seemed to wrap around him. He noticed even the screams had stopped.

The others made no move. Silently they watched him. Renee buried her face in James's shoulder. Bob stared at the ground, only the two officers remained alert, watching Hugo's every move but allowing him time to take in the awful scene.

Dizzy with shock Hugo fell to his knees. Clenching his fists he threw his head back. "Joan!" He cried. On his hands and knees he crawled to her head…the only part of her he could see. The rest of her body lay crushed under Major. Blood oozed from her open mouth. Her dead eyes stared up into his face.

Shocked by his own grief he sobbed quietly. He and his wife Joan Emery Grey had a strange relationship. But from the moment they first met, she had been the only woman in his life. She was always there, loyal, supporting him in everything. They were alike in so many ways, no one else mattered. *It was us against the world*, he thought. Gently he touched her hair. "This place should have been ours," he said softly. "I'm the rightful heir." Raising his head he yelled at the night sky. "Five Acres is mine! It's my inheritance." With a loud sob, his head drooped, his body sagged. He hardly felt the police officer handcuff him and raise him to his feet. Without a word he let them march him to the police car.

ও∼ও∼ও

Renee clung to James, "What's going to happen now?" She asked.

"I'm not sure," James said. "Maybe the officer can tell us." He nodded at the policeman walking towards them. "What do we do now?" He asked.

"I'm sorry, but for the moment I need you all to remain here. More officers and forensics are on their way and they will want statements." He glanced up as Bob walked towards them carrying the shot gun. "I need to take that sir, its evidence."

Bob's eyes glistened with emotion as he handed him the gun, "The horse is still alive, but his front leg is badly broken."

"I'm sorry sir, but you'll have to call out the vet and at the risk of sounding insensitive you need to get him here soon as we need to get to the body."

Major's cries of pain were intermittent and growing weaker.

Taking a grubby handkerchief from his pocket, Bob wiped it across his forehead. "I can't let him lie there, he's in pain. Please, let me put him out of his misery."

The officer took a step back. "I'm not sure sir. It's against procedure."

"Look, it's something I've had to do on numerous occasions. There have been many times I've come across an injured deer or fox." Returning the handkerchief to his pocket he approached the officer. "Please give me the gun. The sooner it's done the sooner you can move the horse's body." Holding out his hand his eyes pleaded with the officer.

"Please, let him do it," Renee cried.

The policeman sighed as he glanced round at his fellow officers. He noticed his boss standing by the gate talking to another man. "Wait here," he said to Bob. "I need to talk to my superior."

Bob nodded, joining James and Renee he shrugged. "I believe he's going to ask his boss."

Renee sighed. "Oh God, I hope he says yes. I can't bear the thought of Major suffering any longer." Renee's voice quivered. Pulling a tissue from her pocket she blew her nose. "Why did that wretched woman have to try and jump Hugo's car. She must have known Major would never make it. It's like she did it on purpose to cause us grief. I'm sorry, but I don't feel any sympathy for her. I know as a Christian I should. But I can't." She stared at Bob and James tears glistening in her eyes. "I ought to feel guilty about it, but I don't!" Her voice rose with anger. Moving away from them she went to Berti. The old horse stood quietly as she buried her face in his mane.

Joining her, James put his arm round her shoulder. "It's okay Renee. We all feel the same at the moment." Sighing he glanced back at the car. "Hugo's a piece of work and he'll pay for what he's done."

Lowering her gaze, Renee rested against him. "I know, but it's like Emery's got away with it. She wasn't supposed to die." Gasping, she pulled away from him. "I've just had a thought. What about the poison? It's the only proof we have."

"Don't worry, I'm sure it's in Emery's pocket and once they've moved Major they will find it."

"But she could have thrown it away when you were chasing her." Gripping his jacket she groaned. "It's the only proof we have. Without it we have nothing!"

James could see the fear in her eyes as she stared up at him. "Look, she didn't have a chance to throw it away. She was too busy trying to escape."

Pulling away, she clenched her fists. "But what if it spilled in the fall, what if it's contaminated. Oh James what are we going to do?"

Holding her by the shoulders James said firmly. "Stop it Renee. Once they are able to search her body they will find it I'm sure, and when they do it will be the end for Hugo."

"I hope you're right," Renee said resting her head on his chest.

Bob walked over to them. "The officer's coming back."

Standing together they watched him approach. He was still holding the shot gun.

"He looks positive," Renee said.

"Let's hope so," Bob said. "We can't leave the horse to suffer for much longer."

The officer joined them. Acknowledging James and Renee with a quick nod he turned to Bob. "Right sir, the boss said its okay." He handed Bob the gun. "However, you can't shoot the animal until we get the lights fixed up and that'll take a good twenty minutes."

Glancing up at the sky Renee sighed. In all the chaos and horror none of them had realised how late it was. Hearing Major's feeble cry she frowned. Under normal circumstances she would be with him...comforting him. But because of Emery's body trapped beneath him no one was allowed near. *I wouldn't want to anyway.* She shivered at the thought.

The policeman took Bob by the arm and led him away from them. "I didn't want to say anything in front of the young lady, but my boss wants to know if you have some way of removing the horse's body?"

Bob's hand trembled slightly as he griped the gun. "Yes, we have a small tractor which is perfectly capable of doing the job." With a sigh, he muttered, "what a mess."

The officer nodded and patted his shoulder. Looking over at the gate, he said. "It looks like the lamps and forensic people have arrived. How soon can you get the tractor here?"

"If it's okay with you I can send my son to get it, and I think Miss Renee should go back to the house. This is all going to be too much for her."

The policeman nodded. "I'll leave that with you sir. I have lamps and a tent to sort out."

"Okay, thanks officer." Calling James and Renee over he explained what the officer had said. "We need to get the tractor up here James, and Miss Renee you need to return to the house. The police will interview us all later."

"That's fine by me," Renee said. "I want to ring the hospital anyway and find out how Cadi is."

James nodded and took her hand. "Good idea."

Renee could feel her cheeks flush. She was grateful for the cover of darkness. Without realising it the awful circumstances had drawn them both together.

Keeping hold of her hand James led her to Berti. "We'll take him back to the stable," he shouted to his dad. "I'll see you shortly with the tractor."

Bob nodded as he walked towards Hugo's car.

Holding Berti on a loose rein, James let the horse amble back to the stables. Renee sat behind him her arms loosely wrapped round his waist. Enjoying her closeness…the warmth of her body, James smiled. "Are you alright?" He asked.

"Considering everything, I'm okay."

Berti's hooves clattered on the cobbles. His pace increased as he neared his stable.

"I think he's glad to be home," Renee said as she slid over his rump to the ground.

"I bet he is," James said. Dismounting, he led the horse into the stable. "I'll see to him. You go and ring the hospital."

"Are you sure?"

James nodded. Going to a switch on the wall he pressed it, flooding the stable with light. "That's better. I can see what I'm doing now." Smiling at Renee, he said. "You go, I won't be long here." Seeing the concern in her eyes as she leaned over the stable door, he asked. "What is it?"

Renee grimaced. "Please, don't forget to tell the police about the poison."

"I will tell them I promise. Now go and ring the hospital."

"Okay, thanks." Spinning round she hurried towards the house. She could feel James watching her. A smile flickered on her lips as she walked away.

Chapter 18

James gave Berti a quick rub down, threw a blanket over him and settled him for the night. "There you are lad enjoy your supper." Going to the horses head he rubbed his nose. "I'm sorry about old Major, you'll miss him and so will I." Patting the horse's neck he switched off the light and bolted the stable door.

The yard lamp cast dark shadows reflecting his mood. Walking to the barn he could see the lights and activity at the main gate. A loud gunshot echoed, breaking the silence of the night. With a sombre shake of the head James opened the barn doors and stood for a moment staring at the grubby old tractor. His chest ached as he reflected on what they were going to use it for.

Dragging a heavy chain from the rear of the barn, he attached it to the back of the tractor and with a weary sigh climbed into the cab. His hands trembled as he turned the key. The old tractor was known to be temperamental. He breathed a huge sigh of relief as the vehicle burst into life.

Leaving the barn he drove towards the main gate dragging the heavy chain. Twisting and turning it snaked along the ground churning up the grass and making enough noise to wake the dead. Seeing his dad waiting by Hugo's car he drove towards him and parked close to Major's body.

"It's done then," he said jumping from the cab.

Bob nodded. "Yeah, we need to remove the tack, but we'll pull him off her first. I can't stand her eyes staring at me."

Seeing his father's grimace, James patted his shoulder, in the artificial light flooding the area he looked pale and drawn. "Come on, let's get this done and go back to the house. I think we both need a stiff drink."

Between them they dragged the chain closer to the horse.

"How long is it likely to take?" An officer asked.

James looked up. "Not long." Ignoring the man they carried on with their work. Securing Majors legs with a heavy leather strap attached to the chain, James climbed into the cab and guided by Bob he drove forward until he took up the tension.

"Okay," Bob shouted. "Keep going."

James pushed hard on the accelerator, for a moment the vehicle didn't move. Looking in the wing mirror he could see his dad urging him on. Grunting, he pushed the accelerator flat to the floor. The engine roared, black smoke billowed from the exhaust. James kept his foot down coaxing the old tractor to take the strain. Gradually, the huge tyres gripped the ground and slowly moved forward. Breathing a sigh of relief, James kept going until his saw his dad waving at him. Stopping the tractor he opened the cab door and jumped down.

Bob ran up to him. "Okay, we're far enough away for them to get on with their work."

The two men watched as police and forensics hurried to Emery's body. In no time a tent went round and people clad in plastic overalls disappeared inside.

Bob couldn't help an involuntary shudder.

"Are you alright?"

Bob shrugged. "As you pulled him off her, the body moved as if she was alive."

Turning away, James shook his head and went to Major. He stared down at the dead animal. He'd known the horse for many years and found it hard to hide his emotions. Scrubbing a hand over his face, James squatted next to the horse and gently patted his neck. "Goodbye old boy, you'll be missed." Feeling his dad's hand on his shoulder he glanced up.

Bob could see the emotion in his son's eyes. "Come on lad the lorry will be here soon. We'd best get this chain off. And remove the saddle and bridle."

James nodded and rose to his feet.

Between them they freed Major's legs and stored the chain in a box at the rear of the tractor.

"How long do you think Frank will be?"

Bob shook his head. "Not long."

As he spoke a lorry appeared, "Looks like he's here. I'm going to have to move my Land Rover it's blocking the gate. You'd best shift the tractor out of the way."

"Okay, I'll take it back to the barn and stay with Renee." Climbing into the cab he remembered the poison. "We need to tell the police Emery could be carrying poison."

"Don't worry, I'll tell them. God willing we'll have the news we want to hear. Tell Renee not to worry." Holding his wrist up to the light he glanced at his watch. "It's getting late, but I'll join you as soon as I can. I just need to help Frank with Major."

James nodded. Grateful he wouldn't have to watch the horse's body manhandled into the lorry.

Conflicting emotions troubled James as he drove the tractor towards the barn. He was glad they'd got Hugo; the man was a nasty piece of work. But for some reason Emery's death saddened him. She wasn't supposed to die. "Or Major," James muttered. Running a hand through his hair he sighed.

Driving the tractor into the barn he parked up. With his head down and his hands in his pockets against the cold, he hurried to the house. Gravel crunched under his feet. As he passed Berti's stable the horse whickered softly. Everything appeared normal, *but it isn't*, he thought. Shaking his head he entered the house and went in search of Renee.

৯৯৯

Renee sat at the kitchen table nursing a mug of hot coffee. She glanced around the room, it felt empty...the whole house felt empty. Sipping her coffee she mulled over her recent conversation with Stella. A slight smile flickered at the corners of her mouth, as she recalled the relief and excitement in Stella's voice.

"Cadi's going to be alright Renee. She's had to undergo blood tests and a stomach pump poor girl, but now she's resting in bed. She's dehydrated so they are giving her plenty of fluids." Hearing Renee's huge sigh of relief, Stella smiled. *"You can relax pet, she's going to be alright. In fact they've said she can come home in a day or two."*

"Oh that's wonderful news Stella. Do they know what it is yet?"

"No they don't, they are doing tests on her blood now. As soon as I know anything I'll ring so don't worry. You try and get some rest."

"I wish I could. It's chaos here. Does Cadi know what's been going on?"

"Not yet, I have to find the right time to tell her. She's too poorly at the moment."

"Don't say anything, Stella. I'll fill you in with the details tomorrow when I come." Renee sniffed and brushed the tears away.

"What is it pet? You sound upset."

163

"I'm alright Stella. It's just the shock of knowing Emery and Major are both dead." Taking an audible breath Renee struggled to control her emotions.

"Are you sure you're alright?"

"Honestly, I'm fine. I'm just so relieved you're there. There are no words to thank you."

"No words needed. I'm here for you both. Now you go and get some rest and I'll see you tomorrow."

Tears of gratitude had flowed freely as she replaced the receiver. If Stella were there she would have hugged her. Wiping the tears from her face she left the table and carried her mug to the sink.

A light tap on the door startled her, she swung round. "Oh James it's you." Waving her hand she motioned for him to sit down. "Would you like a coffee?"

Removing his cap James ran a hand through his hair. "I could do with something stronger but a coffee would be good, thank you." Taking the mug from her, he asked. "Have you spoken to Stella?"

Renee nodded and smiled. "It's great news. Stella said Cadi is going to be fine. They will keep her in for a few days just to be sure."

"Do they know what made her so ill? What was Emery giving her, is it—?"

Rene grinned. "Give me a chance and I'll tell you. Stella said they took some blood and are testing it. She will ring me as soon as she hears anything. Otherwise I'll find out tomorrow when I visit."

James leant back in his chair and sighed. "I'm so glad Cadi is okay."

"Me too, I think we were just in time. Only God knows what Emery was planning. If we had delayed I dread—"

"Don't go there, Renee," James said. "We did the right thing. Okay, we didn't want Emery dead but it's happened. At least we got Hugo." He glanced at the clock on the wall. "Dad should be back soon. He was helping Frank with Major."

Nursing his mug between his hands he glanced at Renee. He could see the question in her eyes. "I'm hoping the police find something on Emery. I'm pretty sure they will. Dad will tell us when he gets here."

Slumping onto a chair Renee leaned her arms on the table. "I pray they find something, if they don't—"

James reached across and touched her hand. "They will, I'm sure of it, and anyway once the hospital finds out what's in Cadi's blood that will be the proof we need."

"True, but the police will want to know whose been poisoning her."

James nodded. "They'll find the proof, so don't worry. That woman was as guilty as sin otherwise she wouldn't have run."

Hearing footsteps they both turned to the door.

"That'll be my dad. We're in the kitchen," James shouted.

Renee watched as Bob took a seat at the table. His flushed face worried her. He looked exhausted. "Are you alright Bob? Would you like a hot drink?" she asked.

Bob nodded. "I'm okay pet. I'd love a cup of tea."

"Coming up," Renee said jumping to her feet. Placing the hot brew in front of him she re-took her seat. As he sipped his tea, she asked him about the poison. "Did the police find anything on Emery?"

Raising his head, Bob stared at them both.

Seeing the smile in his father's eyes, James took an audible breath. "They found something."

"They have. It was a small brown bottle...amazingly undamaged. It's being analysed as we speak. We should know something tomorrow morning."

Renee was speechless. She looked from one to the other, tears streaming down her face.

James took her hand and gently squeezed it. "It's over. We have the proof we need."

Renee sobbed, but James could see the smile...the relief in her eyes. Leaving his chair he took her in his arms. She clung to him. Resting her head on his chest she breathed a sigh of relief.

Watching them Bob grinned. "I think it's time to dry the tears and celebrate. I know there'll be more heartache to go through, but the worst is over."

A little embarrassed, Renee pulled away from James. "You're right Bob. I know where Stella keeps the wine. Would anyone like a glass?"

Going to a small cupboard she opened the door and retrieved a bottle of red. "Is this okay?" She asked. Their enthusiastic nods answered her question.

James took the bottle and pulled the cork, while Renee got the glasses. Standing in a circle they raised their glasses. "To Cadi," they said in unison.

Sipping her drink, Renee closed her eyes and drew a deep breath. The thought of seeing her sister the next morning brought a smile to her face. "Thank you Lord for keeping her safe," she said softly.

Chapter 19

The next morning she woke early to a bright frosty day. Through a gap in the drapes bright sunshine streamed into her room. Scrambling out of bed, Renee padded across to the window and pulled the drapes back. She had grown to love the view...loved the way the light changed according to the weather. This morning the vista resembled a scene from a fairy tale. Overlaid with white frost the trees and vegetation sparkled in the sunlight. Renee smiled, the effect was magical.

From outside she heard voices and the clank of a metal bucket. Glancing at the bedside clock her eyes widened. "Gosh they're up early. I'd better see if they want some breakfast."

Remembering last night brought a warm flush to her cheeks. They had sat around the kitchen table talking and finishing off the wine. Renee was surprised by the strength of her feeling for James. If his response to their kiss outside her bedroom door was anything to go by, she guessed he felt the same.

After all the trauma and upheaval and with the gate blocked by numerous police vehicles, Renee knew they would be unlikely to get home so she invited them to stay the night.

"There's a small twin-bedded room at the back of the house. You're welcome to use it. You must both be tired, I know I am."

Bob nodded, "That's kind of you. I don't know about James," he said glancing at his son. "But I'm tired."

"I'll show you the room," Renee said rising to her feet.

"It's okay pet. Over the years we've both learned the ins and outs of this house. I can find my way, thank you." Clutching his cap he moved towards the door. "I'll say goodnight to you both." Looking at James he smiled and said. "Don't be too long son."

"I won't." James turned to Renee. "You look tired. I'll walk you to your room."

Renee giggled.

"What?"

"Nothing, it's just the idea of being walked to my room as opposed to being walked home. It sounds funny." She smiled at him.

James grinned and took her hand.

Feeling the warmth of his hand Renee blushed. She hoped James didn't notice. They walked in silence up the wide staircase and along the passage until they reached her door.

James stood close…still holding her hand.

Renee could feel his warm breath on her cheek. Raising her head she stared into his eyes. Her stomach fluttered as their lips met. The kiss was tentative…gentle. Breathless, Renee clung to him.

James held her close his heart pounded as she returned his kiss. Pulling away, he held her at arm's length. "I'm sorry Renee, I shouldn't have done that." His voice was hoarse with emotion.

Seeing the blush on his cheeks and obvious embarrassment, Renee pulled him into her arms. "Don't apologise." She gazed up at him. "I feel the same." Seeing his blue eyes crease in a smile she hugged him. "It's late, so I guess we'd better go to bed."

Taking her face between his hands, James gently kissed her on the forehead. "I'll see you in the morning."

Renee nodded. "Thank you for all your help."

James smiled. "You're welcome."

Watching him walk away, Renee sighed and wrapped her arms round her middle. Realising the effect he had on her came as quite a shock. It had been many years since she last fell for someone, and the relationship had ended badly. The remaining scar had left her cautious.

Thinking of James stirred all sorts of emotions. Sighing, she turned away from the window. Shaking her head she tried to put him out of her mind and focus on Cadi. She smiled, knowing her sister was safe and well on the way to recovery, made her feel quite giddy. After all Cadi had been through it was too wonderful for words. Renee felt like dancing round the room. However, seeing the time she pulled herself together and hurried into the shower.

The guys will want some breakfast and I need to get to the hospital. Standing under the hot water humming to herself, she felt the tension of the past few weeks slowly ebb away. She thanked God that soon life would return to some semblance of normality.

❧❧❧

Arriving early at the hospital, Renee was dismayed by the amount of cars trying to find somewhere to park. Forced to join them driving round in circles she could feel her temperature rising. She saw an empty space and drove towards it, but another car coming from the opposite direction nipped into it. Glaring at the driver she accelerated away.

Taking a deep breath she thought, *I need to calm down. This is not a good way to behave.* "Lord, please help me find a parking space." Slowly and with renewed patience she negotiated the car park. There were a few empty spaces, but she was in Bob's old Land Rover as Stella had used her car to get Cadi to the hospital. The Land Rover was large and Renee felt nervous about parking it. Knowing it needed more room than her smaller car.

Fortunately, as she drove around for what seemed like the hundredth time, she spotted a large four by four backing out of a space. Tapping anxiously on the wheel, she waited for it to drive away. Seeing another vehicle approaching she didn't hesitate, manoeuvring into the space she parked up. Breathing a sigh of relief she locked the car and hurried to the main entrance of the hospital. Spotting the information desk she went over.

The young woman behind the desk looked up and smiled. "Can I help you?"

"Yes, I need ward twelve."

"That's on the fourth floor. You'll find the lifts over there," she said pointing.

"Thank you." Following the woman's direction Renee found the lifts. Reaching the required floor she walked along what seemed to be a never ending passage, but eventually she saw the sign for ward twelve. Once inside the usual organized chaos greeted her, and the vague smell she could never quite put her finger on assailed her nostrils. Swallowing the lump in her throat, Renee recalled the painful memories of her mother's time in hospital, with all the upheaval and sadness it entailed.

I need to get Cadi home as soon as possible, she thought. Weaving her way along the narrow passage… avoiding empty beds and busy staff, she made it to the nurse's station. "Excuse me."

The nurse glanced up from her paper work. "Can I help you?"

"Yes please. I'm here to see my sister Cadi Grey."

The nurse smiled and pointed to the small room facing her desk. "You'll find her in there."

"Thanks," Renee said. Walking into the room she saw Stella first. Cadi sat on the bed beaming at her. Renee grinned as she hurried to join them. The three women embraced. Holding Cadi tight Renee let the tears fall, all the tension and horror of the night before surfaced, along with relief that Cadi was safe and would soon be well.

Stella put her arms round them. Both girls were sobbing. She sat on the edge of the bed. There was nothing she could say. After all they'd been through they needed to unburden and let the tears flow. When they calmed down Stella handed out tissues. She watched Renee wipe her eyes. She looked pale and tired. Brushing Renee's hair away from her face she asked gently. "Are you alright?"

Renee nodded. "As alright as I can be under the circumstances." She smiled as Cadi took her hand. "I'm sorry. I didn't mean to get emotional."

"It's the shock of what happened," Cadi said squeezing her hand.

Stella frowned. "You're right. Someone dying wasn't part of the plan."

"That's true," Renee said. "But the plan worked." Gazing at Cadi she noted the touch of pink on her cheeks. "My sister is safe and that's all that matters to me."

Cadi grinned. "I do feel so much better, and should be going home soon." Narrowing her eyes she looked hard at Renee. "Thinking of home is there any more news. What's happening there?"

All eyes were fixed on Renee. Lowering her voice, she said. "The police are still there. They want to speak with me later today. Bob and James have already been interviewed." Chewing her lip she glanced at Stella.

Knowing what she was thinking, Stella nodded, "Go ahead you can tell us everything. After I spoke with you last night I shared what you said with Cadi. I felt she should know."

Renee breathed a sigh of relief. "Good, so you know Major is dead. Emery made him jump Hugo's car, but he crashed onto the roof and fell crushing Emery beneath him. They say she died instantly but poor Major broke his leg along with other injuries." She paused as tears welled in her eyes. "I'll never forget his screams." Looking down at her hands she twisted the soggy tissue. Composing herself she continued. "They found a bottle of poison in Emery's pocket. We're still waiting to hear what it is. I'm hoping we'll know by this afternoon."

Taking Cadi's hand she asked. "Have the Doctors told you anything yet? Do they know what made you so ill?"

Cadi shook her head. "Not yet, but I'm hoping to see a Doctor this morning. I want to know before I leave." Cadi's voice broke as she struggled to control her tears. "I really liked Emery." Her voice rose with anger. Throwing her head back she let the tears flow. "I trusted her!" She cried.

Stella patted her hand. "Don't fret yourself. You weren't to know what she was really like. None of us did."

"Yes, but you had your suspicion, Stella." She looked at them both. "I just didn't want to believe it." Balling her hands into fists, she cried. "Emery killed my husband and she tried to kill me!"

Taking Cadi in her arms Renee sought to comfort her. Her sister's pain tore at her heart. There were no words. Renee knew only time would heal the hurt and anger.

The three of them sat in silence. Stella closed her eyes and prayed silently.

Renee glanced up as the door opened and a young Doctor stood there. "Good morning. I'm Doctor Michaels." Glancing round he could see emotions were high. "If I'm disturbing you I can come back later," he said.

Cadi sat up and wiped her eyes. "No, it's alright. Please tell me what you've found."

The doctor acknowledged Renee and Stella with a polite nod.

"Would you prefer us to leave?" Renee asked.

Cadi grabbed her hand. "No stay, please." She glanced at the doctor. "Is it alright if they stay?"

The doctor smiled. "Of course, if you wish. I have the results of your blood test. It would seem you had a substantial amount of Arsenic in your system. I'm glad you came in when you did. If you had delayed any longer it would have been too late." Lowering his notes, he smiled. "However, the good news is you are clear and once the police have spoken with you, you are free to go home."

Looking at each other, the three of them grinned.

"That's wonderful news," Renee said patting Cadi's shoulder.

"Be sure to rest and take plenty of fluid, and I mean plenty. You need to flush out your system." Doctor Michaels said.

Stella gave Cadi a firm look. "Don't you worry Doctor. I'll make sure she does."

The Doctor nodded. "Good, I'll make a follow up appointment for you just to make sure all is well." Stepping towards the bed he shook Cadi's hand. "Take care of yourself. I'll see you in three weeks." With a friendly smile he left the room.

"He's nice," Cadi said.

Renee and Stella giggled.

"What?" Cadi said, looking from one to the other. "All I said was he's nice."

Still giggling Renee gave her a hug. "I'm so pleased you're better."

"Back to her old self I would say," Stella said.

A loud knock on the door disturbed their happy moment.

Cadi frowned. "That will be the police. You two go and have a coffee," she said flicking her hands towards the door ushering them out. "I'm sure this won't take long."

"Are you sure you'll be alright?" Renee asked.

Cadi nodded.

Stella opened the door and stood aside for the two officers to enter.

As Renee followed her out, she turned. "We'll see you shortly." Cadi smiled but Renee could see the anxiety in her eyes.

ა���

Cadi shivered as she sat in the car watching the landscape flash by. Clutching her hands she played with her fingers. She had not expected to feel so nervous about going home. She'd been desperate to leave the hospital…to return to familiar surroundings, and yet now anxious thoughts cluttered her mind.

Would there be anything to see on the driveway? How would she feel in the house now that Emery was no longer there?

Renee glanced across at her. "You're quiet. Are you okay?"

Cadi gave her a little smile and nodded.

Renee fixed her eyes on the road. "If you're concerned about Stella you don't need to be. She's a good driver and will be fine in the Land Rover."

"I know that's not what's bothering me."

"What then?" Renee asked. Seeing the gates to the estate up ahead she pulled over to the side of the road. "Come on tell me, what's the problem? You've been quiet since leaving the hospital." She studied Cadi, seeing her sister close to tears she reached across and put an arm round her. "What is it? Have the police upset you?"

Staring down at her hands Cadi shook her head. "Only in as much as they told me what happened to Emery." Raising her head she stared at Renee with tear filled eyes. "They said she was crushed beneath Major and suffered massive internal injuries." Pulling a tissue from her pocket she wiped her eyes. "Don't get me wrong, I'm not crying for her. I hate the woman. Even more so when the police confirmed she was poisoning me with Arsenic. If I cry for anyone, it's Major."

Sighing, Renee pulled her closer. "You've been to hell and back. I can't imagine what you are going through." Placing a gentle hand on her cheek she stared into her eyes. "You are not to worry about a thing. It's

175

going to be hard for a while, but I'm here for as long as you need me, and so is Stella."

Resting her head on Renee's shoulder, Cadi sobbed. Through her tears, she asked. "Do you have to leave? This place is huge. Couldn't you stay with me?"

Renee smiled. "I would love to but let's talk about it later, when things are more settled. You still have a bit to face with the court case and inquest."

Cadi nodded, "You're right, but you will think about it?"

"I will, I promise. Now let's get you home. Stella will be wondering where we are."

Leaning against the head rest, Cadi quietly exhaled. Clutching her seat belt she kept her eyes closed. For the moment she couldn't face seeing where it happened. Listening to the tyres crunch on the gravel drive she let the familiar sound sooth her. She was home.

Chapter 20

Two Years Later

Having parked the car, Cadi hurried Renee and Stella to the pub. Due to the heavy rain, Wooler high street was quiet. The three of them laughed as they took off their wet coats. "My goodness," Stella said. "It's dreadful out there today."

"You two take a seat," Renee said. "I'll go and order the drinks."

"Champagne I think," Cadi called after her.

Renee glanced back. "Are you serious?"

"Absolutely, and I'm paying."

"If you're sure," Renee said.

Stella frowned. "That's too expensive pet."

"Order it," Cadi said to Renee.

Pulling out a chair for Stella, she smiled. "With the news we've just had I would buy a crate of the stuff."

Stella laughed. "Okay you deserve it."

"We all do Stella." Sitting down she brushed a hand through her damp hair. "We'll get a cab home. I'm sure James won't mind picking up the car."

"The landlord is happy," Renee said plonking herself in the chair next to Cadi. "I don't think he gets many requests for champagne."

"No I bet, but then I don't suppose he's ever been slowly poisoned. So he doesn't know how awesome it feels to hear the perpetrator has been given life without parole for the crime."

Stella leaned forward and pursed her lips. "Why has it taken so long to reach this point? What with the inquest and all, it's been a torrid time for you Cadi."

Renee nodded. "For some reason it always takes ages for anything to reach court."

Cadi sighed. "I'm just glad we didn't have to keep making that awful journey down to London. I was so relieved when my lawyer said I didn't need to be there for the summing up and sentencing; unless I really wanted to, which I didn't." Seeing the landlord come towards them with a bottle of champagne in an ice bucket they changed the subject.

"This is the best we have," he said apologetically. "Celebrating?" he asked. Their enthusiastic nods made him smile. "Well congratulations. The evil swine got what he deserved. He'll never see the light of day again. Shall I pop the cork for you?"

"Yes please," Cadi said.

"Enjoy," He said as he returned to the bar.

"I suppose the whole area knows now. It's nice having everyone's support, but I don't like my private business open for all to see."

Stella shook her head. "It can't be helped I'm afraid, but don't worry, with the pace life goes at these days it will soon be old news. You concentrate on getting your life back on track." She smiled across at Renee. "Your sister and I are here to help you."

Pressing her fingers to her lips Cady nodded. Her voice broke as she said softly. "I can't believe you're both going to stay with me." A tear trickled down her cheek. "I'm so grateful. I don't think I could stay at Five Acres by myself. Too many memories and yet I would never want to leave."

"Well you don't have to. You're stuck with Stella and me for the long haul."

"Indeed you are," Stella said. "Having stayed with you for all this time, I would be lonely in my own house with no one to cook and clean for." Grinning, she rubbed her hands together. "I'm looking forward to selling my house and making my home with both of you."

"Awesome," Cadi said raising her glass. "Here's to us."

❧❧❧

Leaning back in the deck chair, Renee relaxed in the early spring sunshine. Sighing with contentment, she pondered on how quickly the weeks had flown by. It seemed like yesterday they were drinking celebratory champagne in the pub. In that short time, Stella had sold her house and moved into Five Acres permanently.

Renee smiled as she thought about the letter she had received earlier that morning. A week ago an offer had been made on her own house which she had accepted. In the letter the solicitor informed her that her house was now sold and he needed her to sign the relevant paperwork. Breakfast passed in a blur of happy relief, as they all discussed Renee's good news.

Her smile of contentment widened as she reflected on Cadi's response. She had almost danced back to the table with the hot toast.

"I'm so pleased," she'd said, dropping it onto a plate in the middle of the table. "This must be the happiest house in the whole of Northumberland."

James had seconded her comment as he took a slice of toast and winked at Renee.

Enjoying the warmth of the sun she stretched her arms behind her head. Thinking of James brought a flush to her cheeks.

Since his dad's semi-retirement; James had allowed himself to be coerced by Cadi into moving into

179

the small cottage situated near the stable yard. Renee grinned. Coerced was perhaps too strong a word as he agreed to the idea quite readily. Cadi needed a man on the estate and had offered him permanent work.

Hearing footsteps, Renee sat up and glanced round. It was Cadi carrying a tea tray.

"I thought you might like a drink," she said placing the tray on the wrought iron table. "Shall I be mother?"

Renee smiled and took the cup from her. "I can hear a lot of banging."

"It's James, I've asked him to check the state of the barn as I'm considering turning it into an indoor school. If he says it's okay I'll get in touch with the contractors. It will be a big job, too much for him to do alone."

"Oh wow! That's great. So you were serious when you said you wanted to start a livery stable?"

Cadi nodded. "You know I've been spending a lot of time in Ted's small room. Well, I found some documents they were tucked at the back of his safe," Pausing, she took a sip of her tea.

Renee watched her, trying to be patient.

Cadi smiled at the expectant look on her sister's face.

"Come on, don't keep me in suspense." Renee said. "What did you find?"

"Ted had some stocks and shares, which turned out to be worth a lot of money."

Renee's eyes widened when she heard the amount. "Phew! I don't believe it."

"It's true. I've already spoken to my solicitor. I've made an appointment to see him tomorrow. Will you come with me?"

In a state of shock Renee could hardly speak. "Of course I will. Oh Cadi, I'm so pleased for you."

"Not just me Renee. It's for all of us. You, Me, Stella, and James, we're all family now. Along with the livery stables, this money will help to keep the estate running. And who knows in the future we could have holiday lets. We'll discuss it with the others over dinner tonight."

❧ ❧ ❧

Glancing at her watch Cadi reached across and took Renee's hand. "I think the new horse should arrive soon."

"I can't wait to see him again," Renee said. "I really liked him and he was so nice to ride."

"Come on then," Cadi said, pulling her out of the deck chair.

Passing the barn on the way to the yard they popped their heads in. They could see James at the far end testing planks of wood.

"How does it look?" Cadi asked him.

James wandered over to them. "Not too bad. Most of the wood and especially the supporting struts are in good condition. Once it's properly converted it will make a good indoor school."

Cadi clapped her hands. "That's great news. Shall I book the contractors?"

James nodded. "Why not, the sooner we start the sooner we finish." Removing his cap he ran a hand through his hair. "While this is being done I can finish off that last stable."

"You've done really well, James," Renee said. "Those old outbuildings make great stables."

James returned her smile. "Yeh they do." Cocking his head he listened. "I hear a lorry. I think your horse has arrived."

Bubbling with excitement Cadi and Renee followed him to the yard. James rushed to assist the driver as he reversed the vehicle close to the stables. Cadi greeted the driver as he jumped from the cab.

"Afternoon Mr Wyndom. How was the journey? Is King alright?"

"He's fine Mrs Grey. He always travels well."

As if to confirm his words, loud snorts and foot stomping could be heard inside the truck.

Wyndom chuckled. "He's keen to get out and see his new home." With James's help he lowered the back of the trailer and pulled the gate aside.

Renee's heart fluttered as she gazed at the big grey hunter. "He's beautiful," she said clutching Cadi's hand.

"He certainly is." Cadi pulled Renee aside, so that Wyndom could lead the horse out of the trailer.

The horse's hooves clattered on the cobbled yard. Berti's head appeared over his stable door, his dark eyes bright with interest. Shaking his head the old horse snorted a greeting.

"He's arrived then," Stella said, joining them.

Renee grinned. "Isn't he gorgeous?"

"I don't know much about horses pet, but as long as you're happy," she said, patting Renee's arm.

"Oh we are," Renee said.

Cadi beckoned to her. "Come and say hello to him."

Renee quietly approached the horse. Stretching his neck he nuzzled her outstretched hand. "Good boy," Renee said softly. Staring into his large brown eyes she smiled.

Cadi handed her the lead rein. "We'll put him in this stable next to Berti. They'll be company for each other."

"Good idea," Renee said. Guiding King into the stable she removed his halter and stood for a moment in the doorway watching him. He was a good fifteen hands but gentle for his size. Turning to Cadi, she smiled. "He has a lovely head and kind eyes."

Cadi nodded. "He's gorgeous…perfect for you."

Renee stared at her open mouthed. "Me!"

Cadi grinned. "Yes, King is my gift to you. I remember when we were kids you always wanted your own horse. Poor mum, she got so fed with your constant pestering."

Half crying, half laughing, Renee embraced her sister. "It's too much Cadi. I can't accept this."

"You have to," Cadi said. "After all you've done for me it's my thank you."

"It's a mighty big thank you," Renee said. She saw tears well in her sister eyes as she glanced at Stella and James.

"Thank you is inadequate. There are no words," Cadi said. Facing Renee she returned her gaze. "If it weren't for all of you I would not be standing here now." Her tears overflowed as Renee embraced her. Feeling a gentle nudge on her back Renee looked round and couldn't help giggling.

King was standing close behind her watching them. Shaking his head he whickered softly.

Wiping her eyes, Cadi grinned. "I think he likes you."

"I hope so," Renee said. "Shall we leave him to settle in? He's had a long journey." Bolting the stable door Renee followed her sister into the house. "It sounds like everyone's in the kitchen," she said.

"There you are," Stella said as they opened the door. "Mr Wyndom fancied a cup of tea before he starts back."

"So did I," James said with a grin.

"The horse settled all right?" Wyndom asked.

Cadi smiled at him and nodded. "Thanks for bringing him. You're welcome to stay for dinner."

Wyndom shook his head. "Kind of you, but I need to get back."

"I understand," Cadi said. "Remember me to Mrs Wyndom."

"I will, thanks for the tea."

"I'll come out with you," James said, rising to his feet.

"He's not one for small talk, that Mr Wyndom." Stella said with a chuckle. Handing Cadi and Renee mugs of tea, she joined them at the table.

Leaning across the table, Cadi smiled at her. "This evening Stella, over dinner. I would like to discuss my future plans for Five Acres."

"That includes James," Renee said.

Stella nodded. "I'll have the meal ready for seven on the dot."

"Great, thanks." Pushing her chair back Cadi stood. "If no one minds I'm going to sit in the library."

"You carry on pet. I have work to do in here."

"I'm going out to check on King. I'll see you both later," Renee said.

Stella smiled as she watched them leave. Humming to herself she cleared the table and put the pots in the sink. Raising her head she gazed out of the window. The sun was shining. She could hear a blackbird singing in the apple tree. With a happy sigh she wiped the soap suds off her hands and filled a small bowl with potatoes and carrots. Relaxing at the table she peeled them, ready for the evening meal.

Who would have thought I would be happy selling my home to live here. It was a risk, but I'm glad I did it. Her lips twitched in a smile as she stared round at the kitchen. "I love this room," she said softly. *Actually, I love this house and everyone in it.* Taking a large carrot she sang softly to herself as she peeled and chopped it into the pot.

Chapter 21

Renee leaned over the half door and watched King pull hay out of the net. A hand touching her shoulder made her jump. She swung round, "James you scared me."

James laughed. "Sorry miss skitty." Putting his arm round her he leaned on the door alongside her. "He's a beauty. Are you pleased?"

"Pleased is an understatement. I can't believe he's mine."

"Well he is."

She turned to face him. "Did you know about this?" Seeing his sheepish expression she frowned at him.

"Well you didn't expect me to say anything did you? Cadi has become a good friend, someone I care about, but she's also my employer." Raising his brows he shook his head. "If she tells me something in secret then a secret it remains." Rising to his full height he stared down at her. "Would you not expect the same courtesy?"

Seeing the wicked twinkle in his eye, she punched him. "Yes I would," she snapped at him.

"Very well then," he said. Laughing he grabbed her in his arms. "Do you have a secret you wish to share?"

Renee could feel the heat rise on her cheeks. Gazing into his face she saw the warmth and passion in his eyes.

In a voice hoarse with emotion, he said softly. "I feel the same. I did from the moment I first saw you."

Resting her head against his chest Renee struggled to quiet her racing heart.

James put a gentle hand under her chin. Raising her head, he let his lips brush hers. His kiss was passionate but gentle.

Renee clung to him. She felt she would explode with happiness. She knew selling her home to move in with Cadi was a risk, but they'd always been close. And all the heartache and horror with Emery had strengthened their relationship.

"I'm so glad I left my home to come here." She glanced around. "Five Acres is a beautiful place to live." She stared into James smiling eyes. "If I hadn't come I would never have met you. I'm so glad I did."

James smiled and held her close. "Me too," he said softly.

They were so engrossed with each other they didn't notice King had moved to the door. They laughed as he snorted and nudged them.

"I think he wants to stretch his legs," James said.

Renee nodded. "Let's put his halter on and walk him out to the park. I'm sure he'd enjoy a little grass."

ლლლ

Cadi stood in the quiet of the library. *I love this room.* Staring round she wiped away a tear. "Oh Ted, even now after all this time I feel you close to me." Walking to her husband's desk she brushed a hand lightly over the polished surface. "I miss you so much," she whispered into the silence.

Closing her eyes Cadi took a deep breath. "But you have been avenged my darling, and so have I."

Pulling a hanky from her pocket she wiped her eyes. Raising her head she thanked God for all He'd done and for the three people she loved most in the world.

Hearing voices she walked over to the window. Renee and James walked hand in hand towards the open park land. Their laughter carried on the still evening air. Held on a loose rein King followed them like a patient dog out for a walk. Cadi smiled as she watched them.

Looking up at the sky her eyes widened. *How beautiful it is.* The glorious colours of the setting sun reflected on the soft clouds. The fiery hues took her breath away. Perching on the deep windowsill she watched her sister and James…sitting together on the grass with King grazing beside them.

All of a sudden her mouth fell open as she saw James get to his feet, drop to one knee and take Renee's hand. In a daze Cadi watched them. Her smile widened as she realized he was proposing to her sister. It was a scene she determined to fix in her memory. Resting her head against the wooden window frame, she sighed and closed her eyes. *I'm so happy for them.*

However, a gentle knock on the door disturbed her contentment. Raising her head she greeted Stella. In the dim light it was hard to see the housekeeper's expression. But each tentative step the housekeeper took filled Cadi with trepidation. Something was wrong.

Leaving her seat Cadi hurried across to her. "What is it Stella?"

"I may have misheard," Stella said ringing her hands.

Taking the trembling woman gently by the arm, Cadi guided her to a chair. "Now tell me what's upset you?"

Stella sat stiffly in her seat her eyes focused on her lap. Turning her head she stared at Cadi and took one of her hands.

Cadi could feel her trembling. "Please Stella what is it? Tell me. You're scaring me."

"I'm sorry pet," Stella said. Sitting up straight she took a deep breath. "You know I always watch TV while I prepare the dinner."

Cadi nodded impatient for her to continue.

"Well the news was on, and I couldn't believe what I was hearing." Pausing she put her hands to her face. "They said that awful man Hugo Grey is fighting for parole, going on about his human rights. As far as I'm concerned he's forfeited any rights he might have had."

Seeing Stella's flushed cheeks and fisted hands, Cadi put an arm round her tense shoulders. "Don't upset yourself I'll ring Mac, my solicitor. He will know what's happening."

"How can you be so calm?"

"I'm not Stella. But I was warned this is what would happen."

"But we were told he was going to prison for life," Stella said.

"I know and he is so don't you worry. Let me make the call and put our minds at rest." Sitting at the desk her hand trembled as she picked up the phone. She was about to dial the number when Renee and James came in. Raising her hand, she said. "I'm ringing my solicitor. Stella will explain."

Sitting beside Stella, Renee and James could see she had been crying.

Renee took her hand. "What's happened?"

"I was watching the news and a picture of Hugo came on the screen. It seems he's fighting for parole."

Shaking her head, Renee fiddled with her necklace. "Can he do that?" She asked James.

Frowning, he shrugged his shoulders. "I'm not sure. I would have thought life meant life."

"Me too," Renee said. She looked across at her sister deep in conversation. Watching her, Renee felt her spirit lift a little. Cadi's demeanour seemed relaxed. In fact, as she put the phone down she smiled.

Cadi hurried across to them and sat down. Leaning forward in her chair she told them what the solicitor had said. "We are not to worry. Mac says periodically Hugo will try for parole sighting good behaviour. However, his request will be denied. Mac assured me that in this case life is life. There will be no parole."

Stella's loud sigh brought a smile to their faces. "Thank God," she said.

"Yes indeed," Cadi said. "Let's go and have dinner. We have future plans to discuss." She watched James guide Stella to the door.

Renee followed, but for a moment paused and turned. "Are you alright?" She asked softly.

Cadi nodded. "I am now." She held out her hand.

Renee went to her. Taking her outstretched hand she gently squeezed it. "Don't worry he'll never get to you again."

Seeing the determined look in her sister's eyes reassured Cadi. "Thanks Renee. I can't tell you how grateful I am to have you here." Embracing her sister she said softly. "I love you."

"I love you too, we all do." Renee took a deep breath. "Actually, I have something to tell you and I wanted you to be the first to know."

"I already know, congratulations."

"How do you know?" Renee's brows rose as she watched her sister's cheeks flush pink.

Recalling them sitting on the grass together, Cadi grinned. "I just had a feeling. Not only that, James was smitten the first time he saw you. So when I saw him propose to you earlier in the park, it came as no surprise." Throwing her arms round Renee, she said softly. "I'm so happy for you both."

"Thank you," Renee said.

Separating, they stood for a moment in companionable silence. Hand in hand they stared up at the painting. In the soft light of a lone lamp the door looked welcoming…the vague figure in the window more distinct.

Cadi sighed deeply.

Renee looked at her. "Are you alright?"

Cadi nodded. "I just love this painting. And do you know what? The door looks closed."

The End

About the Author

Biography Y I Lee was born in Swindon Wiltshire, the eldest of three children. From a young age her greatest joy was to curl up with a good book. They became her escape from a troubled childhood. Over time she naturally progressed into writing. At the age of ten, she ambitiously attempted her first novel but quickly gave up. However, the seed was planted, and in the coming years in between a successful singing career she continued to put pen to paper, writing poetry and short stories.

She's always had a great love for animals, especially horses. And thanks to a friend, she also grew to love Fancy rats, and spent a number of happy years breeding and showing them. Understandably, horses and rats often find their way into her books.

Y I Lee and her husband Keith live in the UK, in the beautiful county of Warwickshire.

More Books By Y I Lee

The Shadowed Valley
Through a Glass
Through a Glass : Gathering Storm
A Rat and a Ransom
Rat Run
The Door

Acknowledgments

First and foremost, I thank God, who is the inspiration and encouragement for every book I write. I couldn't do it without Him.

My grateful thanks and appreciation go to David and Ruth Rhodes. Your input and editing skills are invaluable.

I would also like to thank, Jo Harrison for her brilliant formatting. I wouldn't be able to publish without her.

And grateful thanks to Rebecca Fyfe for the awesome book cover design.

Last but not least, I thank my husband, Keith, for his unwavering support and encouragement.

25390536R00112

Printed in Poland
by Amazon Fulfillment
Poland Sp. z o.o., Wrocław